The Purgatory Press
&
After the End

The Purgatory Press
&
After the End

John Culbert

PERFECT
EDGE
BOOKS

Winchester, UK
Washington, USA

First published by Perfect Edge Books, 2013
Perfect Edge Books is an imprint of John Hunt Publishing Ltd., Laurel House, Station Approach,
Alresford, Hants, SO24 9JH, UK
office1@jhpbooks.net
www.johnhuntpublishing.com
www.perfectedgebooks.com

For distributor details and how to order please visit the 'Ordering' section on our website.

Text copyright: John Culbert 2013

ISBN: 978 1 78279 061 7

A CIP catalogue record for this book is available from the British Library.

Design: Stuart Davies

Printed and bound by CPI Group (UK) Ltd, Croydon, CR0 4YY

We operate a distinctive and ethical publishing philosophy in all
areas of our business, from our global network of authors to
production and worldwide distribution.

CONTENTS

For Dina

Lost at sea (consider including a *how* and *why*).

André Gide

The Purgatory Press

The Purgatory Press is ceasing operations. The following titles are available from our backlist.

Michael Harrow, *My Life*

Mike Harrow's reputation as a writer rests on a single slim volume found among the author's effects following his death at the age of 56. A well-known figure in the art circles of Baltimore, Maryland, Harrow often spoke to friends of writing an autobiography. What they discovered after his passing is this strange and remarkable work, totaling a mere ten pages, that contains his entire life story. Harrow's preface describes his aims and inspiration, and its lyrical beauty hints at the writer's secret talents.

A schoolgirl's drawers sometimes hide a picture with a face marked out. A lone portrait or a face among others, but a pen's blot has covered it up. To know and to choose: skills honed in the grind of standardized tests, later in the privacy of the election booth. Here the blot speaks of a passion to obliterate. And behind that passion, of course, is a former love, a friendship betrayed, rivalry, shame. Mingling with a heady smell of ink (ii).

Each chapter of Harrow's autobiography is only one page long and consists of a "blot" such as he describes above. This black mark is the trace left by each letter of every word the author wrote, one on top of the other. The result is of course illegible; the reader is left in perplexity before a text that can be viewed in a glance but defies the eye, a pupil staring back. Should we read these blots as a vengeful act of destruction like the pique of Harrow's schoolgirl? Do they hide secrets Harrow felt unable to share? Such grim speculations are countered, however, by the playful tone introducing the chapters, whose titles, in the

3

manner of the 18th-century picaresque, provide a synopsis of what purportedly follows. Chapter 3, for instance, is jauntily titled, "In which the Author Learns the Pleasures of Competition and Sportsmanship; Reflections on their Use in Later Life."

Just as they defy reading, these chapters resist categorization; the pages of *My Life* were first mounted in a graphic art exhibit at The Drawing Center in New York and traveled on to shows in London and Barcelona. The catalogue for the exhibit included essays by art critics who made great claims for Harrow's experimental style. Alison Ormond-Peña writes, "Harrow's black spots seem like an exercise in negation; no image, no line, no color. But this negation is like the force of a black hole, fatally attractive and leading to other realms of creative imagination." Less grandly, Mark Ehrens sees Harrow's work as a potent commentary on memory in the digital age. "We are used to the idea that our most cherished things can be stored in a flash drive held in the palm of our hand," he says. "Harrow provides an unsettling image of that archive, always corruptible and invisible to the naked eye." Danika Müller's "Harrowing the Field of Vision" is perhaps the most interesting of these essays. Pointing out that the word "harrow" refers to a method of plowing, Müller draws on Martin Heidegger's "Origin of the Work of Art" to bring out what the philosopher calls the *Riss* (a "cleft" or "fissure") at the heart of creative expression. Further, Müller makes use of Jacques Derrida's theory of the *trace* to argue that Harrow's work is quintessentially deconstructive. "Neither sign, symbol or index, the 'trace' is the primary mark that is always already effaced," Müller declares. "Harrow's blots are an apt figure of that vanishing source of creative work intuited by the philosophy of *Destruktion*. No one has managed better than Harrow to wed the rich furrow of the artist's line to its simultaneous erasure."

Paradoxically enough, Harrow's unreadable autobiography has led to his life's renown. And there are some, moreover, who doubt his blots actually contain any words. "What I remember about Mike," says one of his friends, "is him sitting for hours at the coffee shop. He had a fountain pen, which was different, you know? He'd sit there, dreaming, with his pen on the blotter making stains."

10 pp.

Albert Moss, *Janet Tully-Stevens*

In the Black Hills of South Dakota, between the improbable Mount Rushmore and the seemingly impossible Crazy Horse Memorial, a sheer face of polished granite floats above the pines. At dusk its rectangular shape glows like the immense screen of an abandoned drive-in theater. This unfinished monument is the work of Janet Tully-Stevens, whose fitful, visionary and tragic life is the subject of Albert Moss's new book. To some, Tully-Stevens is the Valerie Solanas of the Western American art scene, an unhinged groupie with delusions of grandeur. To others, she is a contemporary Lou Andreas-Salomé, the underrated and nearly-forgotten muse of an entire artistic generation. Moss clearly leans toward the latter, and his book, a monument in its own right, aims to shift the canon and install Tully-Stevens in her rightful place in the history of American art.

Born in Oakland in 1945, Tully-Stevens practiced performance and conceptual art in the 1960s before turning to earthworks and land art. Companion and lover of such figures as Ed Ruscha, Robert Smithson and Bas Jan Ader, she found unwelcome notoriety in 1974, the year she received a prestigious Guggenheim grant. Rather than fund an art project with her grant money Tully-Stevens decided to use it to murder Robert Smithson, but on the eve of her departure to meet him in Amarillo, Texas, she learned of Smithson's accidental death at the site of his final earthwork. The artist then decided to return the check for her grant money, an act she incorporated into a performance piece: driving her car from San Francisco to the Guggenheim headquarters in New York, she kept her car's left-turn signal blinking for the entire journey. Her account of the trip, *Left Turn* (available from Purgatory Press), tells of the reflections, events and encounters provoked by her performance. Part travelogue, part manifesto, and part visionary lyric, *Left Turn* excoriates the art establishment and signals Tully-Stevens' leave-taking from the art world she had traversed like a comet.

Moss's reassessment of the work of Tully-Stevens is more than the account of a colorful and controversial life, however. The stakes of his book are most apparent in Chapter 3, where Moss highlights the influence of Tully-Stevens on Smithson and the Land Art movement. Tully-Stevens first met Smithson at the time of his Mono Lake Nonsite, a period just prior to Smithson's large earthworks. At Mono Lake Tully-Stevens apparently spoke to Smithson about her own project for nearby Lake Tahoe, titled "Draining Tahoe," which, as the name suggests, would have emptied the mountain lake of its water. The project of course was conceptual in nature, but most significant is Tully-Stevens' startling vision of a swirling vortex at the center of the lake. Drawing on Tully-Stevens' journals and correspondence, as well as on interviews with friends and associates, Moss asserts that this vortex is the likely inspiration for Smithson's own Spiral Jetty. The claim is momentous indeed, as it gives credit to Tully-Stevens for what is arguably the most important work of American art of the post-WWII era.

Moss supports his argument with new and enlightening documents. A previously unpublished sketch of "Draining Tahoe" (41) shows a narrow pier reaching out to a viewing platform at the lip of an enormous whirlpool. The similarity with the Spiral Jetty is striking and sheds light on Tully-Stevens' rivalry with Smithson and her bitter disavowal of the art world. As Moss himself admits, however, one cannot conclusively date this drawing, which could in fact post-date Smithson's most famous work. Fascinating and enigmatic, the sketch of the jetty and vortex leaves the reader suspended in wonder at the sheer force and centripetal pull of Tully-Stevens' life and work.

The name of Tully-Stevens appears occasionally in the margins of Michael Heizer's work as well, which credits her participation in a number of Land Art projects in Arizona and New Mexico. Heizer's private journals of the period are somewhat less generous, though. "Tromp down to Rosario and south to see the Mad Woman in the Dunes. At all costs do not get drawn in..." Elsewhere he slaps her with the moniker "Lady Sisyphus of the grain of sand." These journal entries refer obliquely to Tully-Stevens' preparations for an ambitious project in Mexico's Baja California, where the artist would have sifted the beach to transform a 3-mile stretch of uninhabited coastline into two distinct sections of black and white sand. The project entailed complex negotiations with Mexican authorities and the construction of a massive sifting and separating mechanism commissioned from a local quarrying company. Unfortunately, after two years of work the project was halted due to environmental concerns and the equipment was sold off to a glass-manufacturing firm. At the project site there remain two mounds of sand, one nearly black, the other a stark white, like powdered paint on a gigantic abandoned palette.

The last chapter of Moss's book is devoted to Tully-Stevens' final and unfinished work in the Black Hills, where the artist retreated into near-total seclusion for twenty years. The Black Hills project was conceived as an anti-monument in the heart of the most monumental of American landscapes but was perpetually mired in conflicts with the Bureau of Land Management, the National Parks Service and the Lakota Sioux. Tully-Stevens' sketches, reproduced in Moss's book, show the intended shape of the final project: a square piece of paper like an enormous post-it note, one corner crimped and lifted, is carved into the bare rock face. On the paper, scrawled in the likeness of handwriting, are the words, "Honey, we're out of milk." As Moss says,

> In spite of, or perhaps due to its unfinished form, the Black Hills project is the definitive rejoinder to the presumptuousness of monumentality, including the bloated masculine pretensions of Earth Art. The giant inscription on the cliff invokes the cherished illusions on which this country was built, but deflates the American dream in a mock-monument that makes the "land of milk and honey" a vapid alibi for the prosaic and stunted life of our domesticated landscape (93).

At moments like these, Moss seems to channel Tully-Stevens' rants in *Left Turn*. His anger is most pointed when he takes on the critiques of Tully-Stevens by such artists as Barbara Kruger, who dismissed the Black Hills project as "trite" and "pathetic." As Moss says, however, "Before Kruger, before Jenny Holzer, and before the consecration of graffiti art in the 1980s, Tully-Stevens' riff on milk and honey lambasted our commonplaces and confronted the myths of politics, advertising and media in a feminist guerilla war on language and art" (97). Malicious critics seem to delight in the fact that Tully-Stevens' inscription got only so far as the first two letters, "Ho." One commentator judges that the letters are "the artist's final signature on a futile body of work." Moss retorts, "these letters are illegible, and perhaps should be. Truncated, intentionally or not, they swarm with implications, evoking a dubious 'westward ho,' or perhaps a single syllable of the artist's derisive laugh launched into posterity" (98).

137 pp.

Janet Tully-Stevens, *Left Turn*

First published as a chapbook by the author herself and long out of print, *Left Turn* recounts Janet Tully-Stevens' seminal work of performance art: a journey across the United States by car, left-turn signal blinking for the entire trip. The narrative is a searing monologue, often descending into patent diatribe, part *Season in Hell* and part *On the Road*.

> Imagine a country named "Little Corner of the Earth," or "Pathetic S***hole of the World." Now let's say that country shortens its name, out of convenience, to "The World." Howls of protest. Mockery and rage. But this country enjoys its shorthand name with impunity. "America" the gluttonous, the insatiable, with endless black tongues of asphalt, every mile another neon sign touting precious "vacancy." And every minute another good citizen tells me I'm not turning left (33).

64 pp.

Ann Silton, *Stories for Second Childhood*

Ann Silton's book is the first of its kind: a collection of stories designed for elderly people suffering symptoms of dementia and senility. While she adopts the expression "second childhood" for her title, the author notes that the dementia of the elderly cannot be equated with the mental capacities of the young. For this reason, Silton says, books aimed at children do not address the needs of an audience of advanced age, though they are often seen in hospice libraries and nursing homes.

Readers with elderly parents or those facing the prospect of their own diminished mental capacity may find the premise of *Stories for Second Childhood* to be in questionable taste, possibly even cruel. This would be to misjudge the intent of Silton's book, which casts a frank and clear-eyed look at her readership. Silton addressed this purpose in an interview for the *Times Literary Supplement*.

A French thinker once stated that to philosophize is to learn how to die. One might add it's the point of all writing worth its salt. The Grimms' fairy tales do not shy from this duty, sadly abandoned by most of their followers. Children learn to construct their world with fairy tales' mysterious puzzle-pieces. The working of the elderly mind, however, is fairly the opposite. Forgive the term, but the elderly are occupied with decomposing their history, undoing the puzzle of their life stories.

Accordingly, several of Silton's texts read like stories in reverse: things tend to fall apart, to scatter, to "decompose." In "Lights Out," the character Edna, who calls herself "Enda," is beset with childlike fears when the lights in her room are turned off. Enda's fears, though, are not about monsters in the closet but simply about needing to get up in the middle of the night. "What if she tripped and fell? So many things in the dark: the chair, the dresser, the lamp. And what might be on the floor? Boots, papers, books and glasses, glasses and temples, temples and gardens, gardens and plots, soil, sod, logs, clogs" (12). Enda's jumbled litany hides a deeper worry: that her room may have changed in the dark. Is she in the hospice or in her childhood bedroom? The story evokes the many places she has slept in her life, all of them alike when the lights go out and she is lying in bed. This allows Enda to revisit her past, but she cannot recall everything, there is too much she has "dismembered" (13). Her wandering mind trips over lists of disparate things that, muddled and disordered as they may be, allay her fears with their rhythmic incantation.

In "Alphabet Soup," this incantatory pablum reaches the point of glossolalia. An unnamed character turns his spoon in a bowl, reading his ABCs in a kind of nonsense primer. Unlike a child, the character does not compose words but only blobs of letters destined to become "mash and mush" (28). "No midrash for the mishmash," Silton says, "this masticated mess without message or meaning."

Such "sonorous inanity," to adopt Mallarmé's expression, seems at times to aim at a higher literary purpose than *Stories for Second Childhood* may at first suggest. More than a mere palliative for the fears and anxieties of old age, Silton's book questions language itself as means of knowledge and literary creation. In this respect, Enda's bewilderment may be compared with Proust's meditations at the beginning of *Combray* or the bedridden musings of Beckett's Malone. Likewise, the hopeless midrash of "Alphabet Soup" is surely closer to Beckett's *The Unnamable* than it is to *Hop on Pop*. Faced with the challenge of such disorienting prose, all readers, Silton seems to imply, are like the stupefied amnesiacs of her primary audience.

Stories for Second Childhood is available in standard and large-font editions.

49 pp. / 66 pp.

Sanjay R. Patel, *Nebulae, vol. I.*

Released on the eve of the global recession, Sanjay Patel's *Nebulae* seems in retrospect a strangely prescient document. This catalogue of cloud maps may be the perfect coffee table book for the economic times that followed the real estate meltdown, when profits and properties dissolved into thin air.

The author of *Nebulae* retired at 32 from his Silicon Valley company to take on a series of projects at the intersection of cosmology, art and technology. The first of these works he launched with the help of former members of the San Francisco-based art group Survival Research Labs. Two years in the making, Patel's project was a massive installation in an industrial hangar in San Jose that simulated the speed of the Earth's rotation and orbit around the sun. As such, and despite its elaborate nature and extensive cost, the project aimed to do no more than make manifest the actual velocity of a person standing on the ground.

Buckminster Fuller claimed he could feel the world's motion in a peaceful state of cosmic meditation. In contrast, Patel's work physically assaulted his visitors, provoking a sense of panic that bordered on psychosis. Three shrieking jet engines blew wind at the speed of 1,000 miles per hour, approximating the velocity of the Earth's rotation. Meanwhile, to evoke the planet's orbit around the sun at 67,000 miles per hour, lights brightened and dimmed to simulate the short length of a day at that corresponding velocity. One visitor described the lighting's strobe-effect with a quote from H. G. Wells' *The Time Machine*: "Night followed day like the flapping of a black wing." Harnessed to ropes and clothed in protective gear, visitors crawled like desperate hurricane victims to the sides of the hangar, where, in small protected alcoves, windows like portholes provided a view of the outdoors. E. Clare Agare, a reviewer from *Wired* magazine, describes his state of near-hysteria under the effect of the deafening noise, blasting wind and flashing lights. "Out the window were a chain-link fence and dry weeds standing idle in a sunny expanse of asphalt. I looked on this vision of peace on Earth with almost physical pangs of nostalgia." Unfortunately, due to insurance concerns the installation was closed within a week and soon dismantled. Patel for his part was not disappointed, as he had grown frustrated at being unable to factor into his equations the velocity of our galaxy, itself moving so fast as to be unrepresentable.

The artist turned next to the curious project portrayed in *Nebulae*. The book makes use of the most advanced satellite and computer-imaging technology to provide topographic portraits of unprecedented detail and complexity. Color plates, black-and-white elevations and cross-sections capture the size, scale, depth and relief of cloud features, lending their transient forms the durable likeness of habitable territory. And like the pioneer of an undiscovered realm, the author covers his clouds with place names as if anticipating their future settlement.

The reader will be struck by the seeming futility of this project. Each "map," after all, is the image of a space in motion, and the features named on them can have existed only momentarily. A ridge running in a curve at the end of a wide plain, the pocked hollows of a valley, peaks dissipating in mist, these are evanescent traits. And yet each has its accompanying place name, either indicated on the map or specified in an index, and every map is located not only by its spatial position but by its place in time: Mount St. Helena, CA, 20/07/04, 14:37.24 PST, for instance, for the map on page 12. It is perhaps the naming of features that will most surprise the reader of *Nebulae*, since it attests not only to a seemingly infinite power of invention but a painstaking labor that verges on mania. The author's brief introduction makes the case for this naming.

> Here on Earth there is scarcely a hump on the ground that is not graced with a place name, if only by the kids who play there. Even the features of our moon and neighboring planets are named. No one lives in a place called "Northern rill of chaparral escarpment," and there is no such thing as a typical strato-cumulus. So each cloud deserves more than the language of meteorology, which grants them only abstract terms and categories (3).

When the technocrats at JPL put their mark on Martian territory, the result was a landscape littered with the trivia of the moment: names from TV series, cartoon characters, office in-jokes, household pets. Patel's work of nomination seems a labor of love. The map on page 31, for instance, draws its names from the *Bhagavad Gita* and the landscape of the battlefield at Kurukshetra. The reference is strikingly apt for Patel's project. Like Arjuna the hesitant warrior, Patel stops the passage of time to contemplate the extent of his physical and immaterial domains. The map on page 68 draws on Herodotus' account of Xerxes' invasion of Greece, following cloud features that echo the lay of the land at the straits of the Dardanelles. As related by the chronicles, Xerxes lost precious time building a second bridge to replace the failed one he built across the Hellespont. Patel, however, supplies Xerxes another means of crossing into Europe; with a dam closing the Bosphorus and an isthmus stretching across the straits, new links join the Eastern and Western worlds. It is not clear whether these details are dictated by Patel's data alone, or whether his cloud maps instead propose a reinvention of the chronicles of history, as suggested by his frequent invocation of lost causes, such as that of Metacomet, chief of the Wampanoag, in his failed uprising against the colonists of Massachusetts (57-59).

Given the number of maps he has made and continues to accumulate (31,000 and counting), one may wonder how Patel's work of naming can keep up with his mountains of data. Anyone else in Patel's position would likely draw names from the phone book rather than consult classical histories. His response to an interviewer on this point was laconic: "I make maps during the day and name them at night."

Castles in the sky? There are worse insults. In taking on his work of bold uselessness, Patel seems to have turned his back on the entrepreneurial culture of his more mercenary Silicon Valley peers. Rather than turn a profit on the virtual realm, the author provides lasting documents of uninhabitable, unprofitable and transitory beauty.

487 pp.

George Rafael, *Camino*

It has been a long dry spell from *Finnegans Wake* to George Rafael's *Camino*, should we credit the author's admirers. When the first chapter of *Camino* was published in a literary quarterly, the eminent critic Howard Kinnear hailed the arrival of a book that picked up where Joyce left off, sweeping away the timid vanity of all literature since 1939.

> Ever since Joyce hit that high-water mark no wave has reached so high again, as if the ocean itself had retreated, its waters locked up in swelling Antarcticas. Or perhaps we might wish it had been so. For instead we have heard the lapping of ceaseless tongues, the babel of wanton stories, the tepid prattle of so-called novels of all stripes – postdiluvian mediocrity heaving up a perpetual low tide of shamelessly *readable* scum.

Kinnear's review of *Camino* reads like a belated tract from the heady days of militant modernist avant-gardes, and his salvo launched a debate that still rages on. The critic's use of the words "babel" and "prattle" was calculated to parry the attack of those who, he guessed correctly, would tag Rafael's *Camino* with such terms. For *Camino*, radically advancing Joyce's polyglot idiolect of complex puns, sparkling neologisms and baffling solecisms, is composed entirely of verbal units unrecognized by the English language. The book's sustained linguistic opacity has prompted many to dismiss it as mere garbled nonsense. Sound poets, with whom *Camino* seems to bear at least a passing resemblance, have also pointedly disowned the work. "No music in *Camino*," Susan Dean asserts. "*Scat* maybe, but not how we mean in jazz."

Camino's 300-page alphabetic concatenation begins with a now famous – and notorious – first word, "Abba." The critical literature devoted to this initial word alone rivals the commentary on many authors' entire *oeuvres*. "Abba" consists of the first letters of the alphabet, as is readily apparent, evokes an enclosed rhyme pattern, as in the ABBA scheme of the Petrarchan sonnet, suggests a contracted "abracadabra," as some maintain, but more intriguingly performs a chiastic twist, and perhaps, as others argue, a supplementary inversion that links beginning to end, yet without invoking the somewhat pat symmetry of circular structure. In this word one can immediately gauge Rafael's debt to Joyce, whose inaugural "Riverrun" wends to the end of his novel and back again to the start to enclose the whole in an ever-returning flow. Rafael's "Abba" has been taken as the cipher that defines the structure of *Camino* as a whole, and doing Joyce one better, lends the book the baffling topology of a Moebius strip. Accordingly, an active sub-field of Rafael criticism has advanced a "multidimensional set theory" to study the pattern of paradoxical loops that would enlace all features of *Camino*'s composition. Meanwhile, a revived structuralist movement has noted that *Camino*'s "Abba" artfully begins with the phonetic matrix of articulate speech and argues that the text as a whole constitutes a rebirth of language from as-yet undiscovered first principles of grammar. "We should not be surprised that more than one hasty critic has dubbed *Camino* a 'morass,'" Helen Lukes says. "Rafael's book is truly the grammatical equivalent of the primordial swamp."

Judging from these commentaries one might doubt that many readers have advanced far beyond the book's opening pages, let alone the first word. *Camino*'s famed obscurity is only exacerbated by the author's refusal to provide any insight as to his compositional aims. "I take dictation," Rafael has simply asserted. Michael Ainsley's ambitious monograph *Ell Camino* has gone further than most critics in reconstructing narrative features of the novel, arguing that the book's coded language is based on permutations deriving from the form of the letter "L," seemingly inscribed *in absentia* in the suggestively absent article of the book's title. On this basis, the critic maintains that the book's story is secretly ordered on the principle of the knight's move from the game of chess, which in turn is reflected in larger themes along the book's narrative arc. Ainsley claims to have reconstructed several short but intriguing episodes from *Camino*, all of which involve conquistadors in what appears to be a grand mythopoetic reimagining of pre-Columbian America and the discovery of the New World. In one scene, Rafael embroiders on a well-known piece of California lore: the single seed of grass, presumably fallen from a fold in the clothes of a Spanish conqueror, which took root and eventually spread to cover the entire landscape of the West. In what is either a tour de force of synthetic extrapolation or a case of speculative delirium, the critic draws on the language of heraldry to argue that this scene constitutes a *mise en abyme* of the text's "rhizomatic germ of composition," itself figured within a recursive checkered emblem on the conquistador's armor, leading the reader into tales folded into other tales, each coded, perhaps, according to unknown variations on the knight's move, if not on still other ludic moves and strategies deriving from the game of Go.

Such interpretations are rebutted by Steven Toll, who provides a thoroughgoing assessment of the early critical literature on *Camino* and raises the standard for the camp of critics who doubt that Rafael's book is more than a meaningless prank. As is well known, Kinnear, Rafael's most important defender, passed away shortly after the release of the novel on which he had placed such a heroic mantle. Kinnear's tragic death after a long career as a Joyce scholar has been seen by some as the result of the hectic pace of his writing and lectures when, convinced of the second coming of high modernism, he lent all his energy to the advancement of Rafael's book. Toll's conclusion is different; he argues that when Kinnear first read Rafael he was already suffering the first stages of dementia that would lead to his fatal stroke. The critic's glowing praise of *Camino*, in other words, is the product of a morbid delusion that presaged his demise. Few would dispute that *Camino*'s reputation owes a great deal to Kinnear, but in a withering indictment of the field Toll goes further to say that an entire generation of young opportunists, willfully banking on the critic's authority and even exploiting his name in bad faith, are forging academic careers on the basis of a patent error of judgment.

Neither Rafael's admirers nor his detractors have so far offered conclusive findings on *Camino*, which has led to the sobering picture of a community of critics seemingly expounding on a virtually immaterial object. This is the subject of Jonathan Beall's playful, spirited and possibly facetious essay "No *Camino*," in which the author invokes Roland Barthes' notion of "intransitive writing" – late inheritor of Flaubert's dreamed-of "book about nothing" – to propound the idea of "intransitive commentary." Like Rafael himself, Beall argues, his critics resemble the writer depicted in Escher's engraving of a hand with a pencil drawing another hand, itself paradoxically drawing the first. Beall suggests that we might imagine one of those hands with pencil inverted, erasing what the other continues to write. "The critic's felicity lies in the disillusioned embrace of his pointless labor," Beall says. This cheerful conclusion might seem willfully perverse, were it not that the critic grounds his claims in his own ingenious interpolation on *Camino*'s provocative *incipit*: "Rafael's 'Abba' is a truncated variant on a celebrated line from Dante's *Divine Comedy*," Beall contends. "'Abbandonate ogni speranza, voi ch'entrate.'"

310 pp.

Hugh Conaghan, *Alan Johnson, Outsider Artist*

Behind a squat building on New York's Lower East Side an unlikely work of art was under construction for over sixty years, rising from a narrow garden at the rate of about half an inch per year. In 2004, plans to develop the property put the sculpture at risk, pitting a rich New York developer against neighborhood activists and prominent art critics. What ensued was one of the most dramatic public art controversies in New York since the removal of Richard Serra's *Tilted Arc*. Hugh Conaghan's new book tells the story of this controversy and the man at its center: Alan Snow Johnson, an autistic recluse and self-taught outsider artist.

Johnson's family traces its lineage to illustrious names in the Mohawk Nation, including the famous chiefs John Smoke Johnson and Joseph Brant. The artist is the son of a construction worker who migrated in 1924 from the St. Regis Mohawk reservation to New York City, where he worked on several notable skyscrapers. Following an accident that left him partially crippled, Johnson's father became a house painter then the landlord of properties on the Lower East Side. It is in the backyard of the family home that the young Alan Johnson began the artwork that would lead to his fame. At around the age of eight, playing on the foundation of an abandoned outbuilding, Johnson amused himself by coating the concrete slab with layers of surplus house paint. His parents noted that this activity was a calming influence on the moody child and supplied him with the materials that allowed him to continue his work of painting. They could hardly have foreseen that this work would go on for more than six decades. Painting one layer a day, Johnson devoted his life to adding coat after coat to his slab, which now counts upwards of 22,000 layers.

Johnson's work was a familiar sight to neighbors who could watch his patient and apparently pointless labor from nearby apartments. The artist was also a regular fixture along Houston Street and often in front of Katz's Delicatessen, where he was known as "the squeegee Indian," since he made a modest living cleaning windows of parked cars. Jane Jacobs, author of *The Death and Life of Great American Cities*, once profiled the "squeegee Indian" in a column in *The New York Times*. In a moment of speculative history, Conaghan imagines what might have happened had Jacobs looked beyond Johnson's sidewalk persona and granted him more than his proverbial fifteen minutes. The author suggests that Johnson might have been discovered as a vernacular "action painter," contemporary with the Abstract Expressionists, and particularly with Jackson Pollock. The comparison is warranted, as Johnson tended to splash and drip his paint before smoothing it over his horizontal plane, though Conaghan claims that "Johnson's approach is even more abstract than [Pollock's], since the dynamic gesture of splashing his surface remains an act without artifact. All that remains is a blank surface, but that surface is the concrete embodiment of Johnson's medium, time itself" (39).

Conaghan does not aim to slot Johnson within the action painting movement, however. With time as his medium, Johnson's slab defies the category of painting, while approximating sculpture in its mass and heft. The paint slab might be called a "journal," each layer a page composed in one day, and the art critic suggests that this rigorous commitment to an aesthetic discipline is perhaps more significant than the slab itself. Indeed, the artwork tends to "dematerialize," he says, becoming the prop of a "metaphysical" inquiry into the dimension of time (40). In this light, Johnson's slab is more akin to Arte Povera, while anticipating the immaterial reaches of conceptual and performance art.

These claims are advanced in a stunning way in chapter 4, where Conaghan compares Johnson's "monument to time" to Andy Warhol's 1964 film *Empire*, an uninterrupted 8-hour shot of the Empire State Building. As Conaghan points out, Johnson's father worked briefly on the construction of the Empire State Building in 1927, and this stint entered into Johnson family lore, though with a bitter undertone, as the artist's father was injured at the site. Conaghan argues that Johnson inherited this ambiguous history by raising a monument of his own, one that ascends not heroically, however, but only in incremental layers. When asked how high he aimed to build his slab, Johnson once replied, with characteristic brevity, "to the moon." Parsing the statement, Conaghan says that it suggests not so much lofty ambition as it does a challenge to the vertical thrust of imperial architecture. Indeed, it is from the perspective of a Mohawk that the pretensions of the "Empire State" come most clearly into focus. More pointedly than Warhol's film, Johnson's slab is a mute, stubborn testimony to the passage of time and the vanity of imperial New York.

With the lobbying of a number of high-profile artists, Johnson's work was purchased in 2006 by the planners of the World Trade Center Memorial. The historical resonance of Johnson's work proved irresistible to the planning committee, which recommended its placement at the center of the Ground Zero memorial site. The slab was seen as a dignified symbol of the pancaked buildings and its wrinkled layers of paint a solemn image of the strata of history, pressed thin as if by geological force into a gnomic palimpsest. The media spotlight on Johnson and his family backfired, however, when an interviewer quoted a neighbor who recalled Johnson's father having once said, in reference to the Empire State Building, that he "wished he could have knocked it down" (81). Subsequent protests by the group Families of September 11 put the fate of Johnson's piece in limbo. The slab remains in storage today, while other bidders, including the New Museum and the Dia Art Foundation, have attempted to adopt it. Johnson himself is attracted to the prospect of its purchase by Dia, which intends the piece for its museum in

Beacon, New York. The artist seems pleased that his slab could find its way up the Hudson, though, he adds, it belongs "further North," no doubt meaning in Mohawk territory.

In a final coda to his book, Conaghan points out that recent astronomical findings show that due to the continuous widening of its orbit, the moon is receding from the Earth at a yearly rate of one and a half inches. At its own incremental growth rate of half an inch a year, Alan Johnson's slab never grew closer, then, but only increasingly far from its purported target.

112 pp.

Ryan Baines, *The Case of Thom Cahill*

Thom Cahill was a promising young member of the New York School of poets who had published only a handful of poems when he won a fellowship in 1967 at Yaddo, the famed artists' retreat in Saratoga Springs, New York. Two weeks into his residency at Yaddo, however, Cahill vanished and has never been heard from since. Ryan Baines' book offers a fascinating account of Cahill's work and advances an intriguing theory about the poet's life after his disappearance.

Baines bases his theory on a discovery made in 1999, when highway work crews clearing brush along the I-87 freeway in Saratoga found a makeshift home on the highway median strip. The home was hidden in a dense thicket of brambles and built into an embankment to further obscure it from view. There were signs of recent occupancy but work crews found no one inside. Before it was razed the Saratoga Police Department took photos to document the illegal structure and Baines reproduces these photos to make his case in his book. According to Baines, Thom Cahill would have retreated to this site soon after arriving at Yaddo and spent over thirty years there in total isolation. If true, the case presented by Baines is unusual to the highest degree. The highway median is only 35 feet wide and is located in the middle of one of the busiest North-South axes in the country. Moreover, it is directly across from the eastern edge of the Yaddo property line. After his mysterious disappearance Cahill would have lived a secret life only a stone's throw away from the artists' retreat.

A professor of English and poetry at the University at Albany, Baines has written a book that reads like a mystery novel. His role as literary sleuth begins with a conversation at a bar in Albany, when a retired police officer brings up the strange case of the house in the median strip. The officer happens to mention that among the objects left behind in the dwelling was a sizeable collection of poetry. Out of curiosity, and without yet operating on any hunch, Baines inquires into the case and consults the list of books in the police file, which includes an exhaustive collection of New York School poets, but nothing by Cahill. This absence does not strike Baines until later when he is teaching a course on contemporary American poetry and runs into the name of Cahill, the missing poet. Baines comes to be convinced that the absence of Cahill's work among the collection is a decisive clue, and turning to Cahill's poetry he finds evidence to support the claim that the house in the median strip is the secret work of the poet. Or rather, as Baines has it, the house is itself a work of poetry, a work announced in the fragmentary poems Cahill penned before his disappearance.

Fellow writers recall that among the books that most influenced the young Cahill was Gaston Bachelard's *The Poetics of Space*. A work deriving from phenomenology but drawing extensively on poetry as well, Bachelard's book speaks of lived spaces as reflections of man's poetic nature and seeks to awaken in the reader a sense of poetic dwelling by means of the dreamscapes evoked in literature. Cahill's writings, while urban in character, sought to give form to this theory in poems that described the tenements, gritty streets and housing projects of New York. Baines conjectures that the artists' retreat in Upstate New York could hardly have suited Cahill's work, and this may well have provoked his departure. Why, though, would the poet have isolated himself in such an unusual setting and taken on his anomalous building project?

The answer to these questions, Baines says, may be found in the photos of his dwelling taken by the Saratoga Police. With these pictures Baines has been able to reconstruct the floor plan of a house that was no more than nine feet wide, but which had several rooms in succession, a trap-door to a crawl space, and a walk-up to a sleeping loft under the rafters. The house was constructed of reclaimed materials, mostly wooden pallets, no doubt over an extended period of time. Cahill had tapped into a city streetlight on a highway overpass to supply the dwelling with electricity and had diverted water from irrigation lines for plumbing. A great deal of work went into camouflaging the dwelling, which was partially buried and surrounded by spiny holly and brambles. This work of hiding the dwelling was dictated by the illegal site, of course, but it also reflects a design inspired by *The Poetics of Space*. Baines argues that the house was designed as a symbolic *burrow*, a "den of reveries," as Bachelard puts it, with elements also deriving from the structure of beehives. As such, it evoked the security of the womb while allaying the fears of the underground grave. The den also owed its security to its fortress-like defense against the world. Here the inspiration was less practical than literary; Bachelard cites Robinson Crusoe's makeshift island fort as the eminent literary example of this fantasy made real. Cahill's dwelling would have combined all of these elements, including the "island" of the median strip to make his ideal poetic home. A city-dweller at heart, Cahill did not seek out the wilds to build a home, but instead a site surrounded by the hum of constant traffic.

Baines dwells at length on the burrow's trap-door to the cellar, not only because it completes the necessary elements of Bachelard's house of dreams – basement, ground floor, attic – but because it signals a deliberate effort to create a *crypt* in the home. The author quotes from Bachelard's *Earth and Reveries of Will*: "The house of memory ... is built over the crypt of the oneiric house. Within the crypt we find the root, the bonds, the fathomlessness of dreams. We *lose* ourselves in this dimension; it has an infinity. We dream of it as of a desire, an image that we find sometimes in books." Glossing these insights, if not "losing himself" in Cahill's crypt, Baines says,

> Cahill's early poetry re-enchanted the everyday spaces of the city, but he had a stubborn nostalgia for the ideal poetic homes evoked by Bachelard. His solution to this conflict was not to beat a retreat to the country but to carve out a private niche in a public setting. His island-burrow is a concrete poem that makes tangible the "poetics of space" in his New York poems. Even his disappearance is an act rich in symbolism: he disappeared as artist-in-residence at Yaddo to become instead the artist of his own residence (83).

Only a literary critic could have solved this mystery, if indeed Baines has solved it. For their part, the police consider Cahill an open case of a missing person; being of draft age, the poet may have slipped north into Quebec to avoid conscription. As for the burrow on the median strip, it would be the work of a vagrant who has since moved on.

94 pp.

Sarah Doone, *The Love of Animals*

Thanks to its vocal detractors, *The Love of Animals* has gained notoriety as a libertine apologia for bestiality. But this intelligent and sensitive book is more than a call for the liberation of desire. It may be quite the opposite. For *The Love of Animals* also makes an impassioned but conscientious argument against one of our most stubborn prerogatives, the freedom to kill and eat animals. The author claims that the love of animals and a newfound bestiality can surmount the rivalry of man and beast, and in so doing help define the killing of animals as murder.

> Jean Genet once stated that "only violence will overcome brutality." We are tempted to invert the formula. Genet's principled resistance to cruelty, admirable as it may be, unfortunately marks his enemies with the sign of the *brute*. Here we argue that the beast must be embraced. We thus find ourselves on the side of the animal, and joining with him against a common foe: the violent murderer, not only of our kind, but also his (14).

If this is a manifesto, one fears it can only fall on deaf ears. And yet this burden of incomprehension may be the measure of today's most righteous voices and urgent causes. By giving voice to those who cannot speak, Doone is willing to let that voice carry a message that gets no hearing. Perhaps to speak for animals is to speak in an unauthorized voice that borders on sheer fabrication. This is not to discount the political force of Doone's study, but rather to suggest that politics can gain from the resources of fiction. Indeed, for readers of J.M. Coetzee, *The Love of Animals* will surely call up *The Lives of Animals*, itself a manifesto tucked into a fiction, and authored by animal-rights proponent Elizabeth Costello, lonely exponent of a lost cause, an awkward, stubborn, righteous and intransigent character one could sum up in the word *impossible*.

Doone's credentials, however, are indisputable, and her book ranges widely and authoritatively from Greek mythology and fairy tales to recent philosophy and political theory. Her introduction offers a broad reassessment of our moral and political heritage by questioning the very foundations of taboo and human law. Drawing on psychoanalysis and anthropology, Doone points out that the taboo on incest has been called the original basis of law and the symbolic order; by enforcing marriage rules that foster social exchange between families and across communities, the taboo also establishes the all-important distinction between human and animal society. But a more basic taboo precedes the prohibition of incest, Doone argues. The ban on bestiality, like the incest taboo, responds to an insistent temptation that is only sensed in the inverted affect of disgust.

> Divine, in John Waters' film *Pink Flamingos*, is hungrily following a dog on a leash. When the dog defecates on the sidewalk, she stoops down to eat his turd. This is the supreme act of perversion in a film of legendary perversity. Most viewers are bound to recoil at the sight, though we all participate in the *frisson* of a taboo vicariously transgressed. And yet Divine's stunt is only a small step from the violence of eating an animal, a vice the film slyly holds beyond reproach. Divine the apotropaic. Rather than recoil from the scene, we should instead step away, as if watching from a place more lofty than divinity, to view meat in human teeth as the very depth of moral depravity (29-30).

The chapters of *The Love of Animals* cover such topics as folklore, television animal shows, "stupid pet tricks" and online pornography. The *tour de force* of Doone's book, however, is her chapter on Virginia Woolf, "Twilight Tales: Between Dog and Woolf." Doone shows that canines play an important role in the modernist author's work, and the scholar focuses on a neglected story of Woolf's titled "Flush," the fictional biography of Elizabeth Barrett Browning's pet dog, to argue that the story's theme of trans-species love conveys the latent force of a bestiality both desired and disavowed by the novelist. Doone cites from "Flush": "Between them," Woolf says, "lay the widest gulf that can separate one being from another. ... Thus closely united, thus immensely divided, they gazed at each other" (67). As with other Bloomsbury authors, dogs allow Woolf to explore a range of desires and emotions that fall under sanction in the social milieu of her early 20th-century England. In this way, canines provide a portal to the unconscious and a means for Woolf to compose her celebrated stream-of-consciousness narratives. But Doone argues that dogs and other animals are not so much symbolic stand-ins for unruly desires as they are objects of a stifled passion that runs throughout Woolf's work.

To make this claim is to shift the Freudian optic that has dominated Woolf scholarship and shed new light on a brilliant but troubled life that ended in suicide. Curiously, however, the approach also wards off a queer angle on the author's life and work, as if determined to outstrip all other biographical scandals. Citing from the letters between Leonard Woolf and Virginia, Doone points out that Leonard called his wife "the Brute," while she herself adopted the name of "the Mandrill," and addressed her husband as "my pet." Doone concludes that just as the story of "Flush" provides an animal's perspective on Elizabeth Barrett Browning's marriage, so does it serve as a critique of Woolf's own domestic life. A tragic longing thus marks her marriage, and this longing, more than any other taboo, drives the haunting lyricism of Woolf's sensitive, searching prose.

Woolf's literary voice wells up from an unspoken desire that, due to its asymmetry, will remain always inarticulate. Art makes room for that babbling. But perhaps art is a poor compensation for the unanswered question in "Flush," "could it be that each completed what was dormant in the other?" Burdened with this question Woolf chose to end her life, but she left a warning about the tragic cost of denying an animal's love (84).

189 pp.

Chuck Banning, *Self-Portraits*

Had he lived into this century, Chuck Banning's career would have blossomed. The photographer thrived on catastrophe. We can only imagine him in Iraq in 2003, in New Orleans in 2005, on Wall Street in 2008, in Gaza in 2009. He disappeared, however, on September 11, 2001, attempting to photograph himself in front of the still-burning North Tower of the World Trade Center, no doubt with his signature smile.

Banning gained notoriety after his visits to Sarajevo and Rwanda, where he made the first of his infamous self-portraits. Clad always in a pale blue polo shirt and crisp chinos, the photographer stood with a broad, fatuous and blank smile in front of scenes of the most appalling wretchedness and horror. Of the photographs in this collection, the portraits from Rwanda are the most graphic and unsettling. There Banning benefited, so to speak, from the slow rescue and recovery following the massacres in 1994. In each of these photos, Banning's smile is an obscenity that draws our ire. Is that enjoyment we see on his face? Isn't he smiling in complicity? How else can he present such a look of contentment and self-satisfaction? Our reactions are not aided, on the contrary, by Banning's public persona that is bland, cordial, banal. Like one of Jeff Koons' cheerfully kitsch chrome sculptures, Banning's portraits reflect our own distorted image in their glossy surfaces.

Banning has been called "a glorified ambulance-chaser," "a postmodern Weegee," and "an amoral peddler of kitch horror." Jamaica Kincaid, reviewing Banning's Rwanda portraits in The New Yorker, delivered a withering indictment of his "smug scorn for human lives strewn like the collateral damage of his own conquering vanity." And yet such criticism seems all-too ready to identify Banning the author with the persona pictured in his photographs, an effect Banning himself fostered in his Warhol-like cultivation of a blank public image. One might instead see these photos as impersonal and ironic versions of the mundane spoils of tourism, such as critiqued by Kincaid herself in her essay *A Small Place*. Indeed, they fully corroborate Kincaid's memorably blunt depiction of the typical tourist as "an ugly, empty thing, a stupid thing, a piece of rubbish pausing here and there." As Kincaid has shown, tourists' vacation pleasures exploit the cheapness of life in places they temporarily grace with their dollars. Banning's portraits make such exploitation violently explicit, but by eliciting revulsion they tend to short-circuit our critical judgment. Strangely, in so doing they can make the viewer a kind of tourist; if a tourist is precisely someone who resents other tourists, to hate Banning's smiling face would be a vain reflex of defensive misrecognition and our disgust a blind recoil from the proof of our own voyeuristic privilege.

In November 1998, Banning traveled to Laramie, Wyoming, where a young gay man, Matthew Shepard, had been murdered a month earlier. The hate crime drew national attention and Laramie became the site of heated confrontations between gay rights activists and religious homophobes. The fence where the young man was strung up to die became a meeting place and makeshift shrine for Shepard's friends and supporters. Here Banning took the photo that led to his wider notoriety (32). The picture shows a stretch of fence piled high with a colorful riot of flowers, wreaths, notes of sympathy and protest placards. Several figures by the fence stand and kneel in poses that evoke figures of classical religious iconography, an impression heightened by a glorious backdrop of high clouds and angled shafts of sunlight. A young mother cradles a child, a pietà in overalls; a group near the fence suggests witnesses to the crucifixion. This allegorical dimension combined with the jarring anachronism of contemporary clothing makes Banning's scene resemble a photograph by Jeff Wall. And yet unlike the latter's work this image is not staged; to the left a group of mourners have turned to look in stunned disbelief at Banning's smiling face, while one face among them is directed at the camera, and thus toward the viewer. The image is something of a miracle, and it is surely the photographer's masterpiece. Reflected here among the figures in the scene are our own pious sentiments, our questioning of the artist, and our interrogating gaze. One cannot help feeling that the image is marred only by Banning's vapidly smiling presence. And yet, of course, it is his presence on the scene that made this rich photo possible, orchestrating a complex play of visual perspectives akin to Courbet's reflexive self-portrait *The Painter in his Studio*. And like Courbet's allegorical painting, it displays an image within an image, a figment within a fiction, an illusion of reality conjured as if by magic by the artist's "conquering vanity."

66 pp.

John Noland, *Zap: A Cultural History of the Sixties*

Some books seem to write themselves, filling an unsuspected void. Once published, they take their place in the library crowned with an air of inevitability. For rivals in the field the instant classic provokes admiration, but also envy. Most galling for jealous readers is the mute self-evidence of the book, its casual persuasiveness, its exasperating superiority, like the unassailable confidence of a handsome face. Why, one asks oneself, didn't I write this book? But perhaps we all did, unawares, unconscious authors of a history we dreamed into writing.

John Noland's *Zap* joins a crowded field of histories of the 1960s but easily shoulders aside the competitors. It offers an exhaustive portrait of the times, and yet its bibliography does not square with the names and sources of its field. Browsing the index of Noland's book is like opening Borges' Chinese encyclopedia, famously invoked at the beginning of Michel Foucault's *The Order of Things*. Borges' parable allowed Foucault to discern in the "hidden network" of order "that which has no existence except in the grid created by a glance, an examination, a language." To explore this historical space, Foucault says, is to uncover "tangled paths, strange places, secret passages, and unexpected communications." Similarly, tracking counterculture in an age of atomic order, Noland disorients our bearings in the cultural archive. He does so with a disarming and seemingly offhand premise: as suggested by the book's laconic title, each chapter revolves around an instance of the phonetic unit *zap*. An encyclopedia, then, limited to the letter Z. This gambit is neither arbitrary nor constraining, though it does provoke unexpected links and strange correspondences in a period of history we may have thought we knew. From Zapruder's film of the Kennedy assassination to Zap Comix, and passing through Frank Zappa, Roy Lichtenstein (*Zap! Pow! Wham!*) and Philip K. Dick (*The Zap Gun*), John Noland's book aims at nothing less than a reinvention of the decade. Hoping the name will stick, his admirers have already dubbed it The Zap Era.

Playful, adventurous and critically acute, Noland draws on the subversive promise of surrealism to show how pop culture has plumbed the depths of the irrational to reinvent a world of desires and possibilities. In his introduction, "Zapping," the author reminds us that the surrealists were fond of randomly walking in and out of theaters to take in disjointed fragments of films. Channel zapping is the modern equivalent of this art of disorientation, which Noland exploits in a collage-like splicing of topics within and between chapters. And yet, siding with the Situationists' critique of surrealism, the scholar is always alert to the co-opting of the unconscious by politics, advertising and media. To avoid these pitfalls, Noland draws on Salvador Dali's maligned "paranoia-criticism" as mode of inquiry, and his phobic, near-psychotic approach to the objects of cultural analysis yields insights beyond the spectrum of conventional politics.

This is nowhere more apparent than in Noland's chapter on Philip K. Dick, "Zap Guns," in which Noland, like a psychotic private dick, follows the trail of his own self writing a chapter on the SF visionary. Gumshoe of his other self, shadowing each sentence with a sadistic and inquisitorial conscience, Noland grips the reader in a kind of claustrophobic paralysis.

> The hollow inside of Dick is like the intangible mold of an empty glove. That glove grips our imagination. But when I turn it inside out, it's me stuck inside that black glove, which I can feel holding a pencil, and scratching away on some hard vellum, a scratching I feel but can't see or hear. Remember those German pencils labeled "dick"? Who's asking? And who asks, who's asking? Two dicks separated by a thin skin. Ask Isadora, no, I don't want to know, and besides, isn't she ghost-written by one of Hefner's pricks...? (87).

Like Neil Bartlett's deeply personal study of Oscar Wilde, *Who Was that Man?*, Noland's sleuthing exhumes the ghost of a great literary forebear, a sacrificial victim who died prematurely in destitution. For Bartlett, Wilde's legacy is vindicated by a history of subversive and illicit gay culture radiating from London worldwide. Noland, for his part, tracking Dick in San Francisco,

San Diego and the wastes of Orange County, sees his author as the voice of homo-panic and the psychotic prophet of Nixon and Reagan's new world order. In this way, panic and paranoia are not simply the reflexes of denial and self-delusion. Rather, with Dick as his guide, Noland suggests that "paranoia is the love of truth, and panic emotion's austerity in a coming brotherhood of human pain" (93).

In *Zap*'s final chapter, "Paz," Noland makes good on this apocalyptic promise. The author traces a political genealogy backward and forward from Dick's ferment of Reaganaut paranoia and the rout of American leftism to the emergence of agrarian revolution among the Mexican Zapatistas – a sci-fi flight of breathtaking speculative history and surrealist time travel.

After Dalì's death, the Spanish artist's paranoia-criticism found stunning confirmation when researchers used advanced X-ray imaging to examine Millet's painting *L'Angélus*. The painting shows two peasants, man and wife, their heads bowed in simple piety in a field at sundown. Dalì had long been obsessed with the painting and was convinced it was hiding a more gruesome meaning. In his mind the wife was a praying mantis pausing for a moment before striking her husband and devouring him, a claim others considered delusional. The researchers, however, found that Dalì had reason to be disturbed by the picture; evidence under the surface of the paint shows that the two figures' heads were bowed over a small grave, presumably that of their own dead child. A stillborn infant or an unwanted child, perhaps, buried in secret by Millet, and haunting the paranoid critic. Every page of Noland's *Zap* offers an image such as this, emerging from the text of history like a secret watermark.

186 pp.

Eric Radiswill, *Masks of the Ceremony*

Eric Radiswill's book sheds light on a long-neglected work of anthropology and the secret research of its author, Raymond Coombes. A specialist in the art and culture of the Northwest Coast Indians of British Columbia, Coombes came to precocious notoriety at the age of 30 with his Ph.D. dissertation of 1954, provocatively titled "Introduction to the Work of Mickey Mouse." Echoing the title of Lévi-Strauss' seminal study on Marcel Mauss, the father of French anthropology, Coombes' irreverent thesis challenged the premises of structuralism and anticipated later strains of cultural and political anthropology by arguing for the study of contemporary mass culture as a means to grasp emergent patterns of sexuality, kinship and social exchange. In spite of the splash caused by his "Mickey Mouse," however, Coombes' highly-anticipated first monograph, simply titled *Mask*, would not see the day until decades later. *Mask* is the fruit of a quarter century's research Coombes conducted on the famous masks, costumes and ritual ceremonies of the Haida, Tlingit, Tsimshian and Kwakwaka'wakw Indian bands. While based primarily on fieldwork and archival research among the First Nations, *Mask* also ranges widely across anthropology and history, from Japanese Noh drama to West African funerary rites, and from tropical bird plumage to drag and transsexuality. As stated in its opening pages, Coombes' book aims at nothing short of a comprehensive theory of the arts of masquerade and dissimulation. And yet *Mask* is a remarkably brief text, and upon its release the book was seen to fall well short of the grand synthetic claims outlined in its ambitious introduction. Defenders of the book took it as a promising first volume of a larger body of work that proved to be never forthcoming. Greeted with passable reviews, *Mask* gradually faded into obscurity. According to Radiswill, however, *Mask* is itself an exercise in dissimulation, and its perceived failings in fact a ruse. Radiswill claims that within Coombes' book are hidden the traces of another text the author never put into writing.

When Coombes died, colleagues and researchers expected to uncover a wealth of ethnographic data in the bachelor's home and office. Instead they found only a standard library of anthropological tomes and professional journals. All of the scholar's field notes were missing, apparently destroyed. There were no drafts of unpublished texts; even the manuscript for *Mask* had gone missing. The only evidence of Coombes' fieldwork was a single cassette tape Radiswill unearthed from among Coombes' collection of classical music. Radiswill believes that Coombes made a concerted effort to eradicate his history among the First Nations, and the lone cassette escaped his purging only by chance. *Masks of the Ceremony* is largely based on the evidence Radiswill collected from this rescued tape.

The story Radiswill tells in *Masks of the Ceremony* dates back to the late 19th century, when the Canadian government banned a longstanding tradition of the coast tribes, the potlatch. A grand and ostentatious festival, the potlatch marked important occasions and celebrated the bounty of the native world, sometimes culminating in the ceremonial destruction of vast sums of wealth. Whites saw the potlatch as an offense to morality and the modern economic values of thrift, productivity and commercial exchange; "senseless," "profligate," "wasteful" and "useless" were epithets commonly used to militate against the practice. A period of demoralization and cultural decline followed the potlatch ban, proving the law's canny force as a decisive weapon in the whites' long war of colonization and ethnocide. It was not until 1951 that the law was finally repealed, at which time the potlatch was reclaimed by resurgent First Nations, but with limited success and on a much smaller scale. Meanwhile, another ceremonial practice emerged among the tribes, this time in hiding, however. Coombes was apparently the only outsider privy to these new ritual activities.

As Radiswill recounts it, the new festival was a celebration of the fall harvest and a preparation for the winter months. Taking place as it did in October, it replaced the Canadian holiday of Thanksgiving, a replacement rich in symbolism, Radiswill points out, as the historic feasts the holiday commemorates are remembered among the First Nations as a bitter prelude to their betrayal by the whites. The new festival was not merely a return to former traditions, however, but borrowed from contemporary customs in using modern equipment and amenities. Each festival was closed to outside bands and carried out in secret.

For weeks the village hummed with busy preparations. Men hunted and fished, and women gathered to prepare the bounty in an enormous feast. A festive spirit imbued all the tribe's activities: smoking the salmon, weaving ceremonial dresses, carving masks and making costumes, building great processional floats for a street parade. Each year a new banquet hall was built from scratch, and the sound of hammers and saws merged with the voices of the singing cooks in a constant symphony (74).

As the work drew to a close, however, the festival took a surprising turn.

The final preparations were carefully timed. When the pots of stew were fully seasoned and piping hot, they were not ladled into bowls but put into Mason jars and tins. As a mother finished sewing the collar of an elaborate costume, her daughter would begin unstringing the beads, unweaving the hem, and rolling the thread back onto spools. The ceremonial float, garlanded in showy flowers, was nearly complete and ready for the parade; as the decorator applied the finishing touches to the front, a crew began work dismantling it from the back. A month's work was quickly dispatched in an orderly and businesslike manner (96).

After weeks of planning, in other words, the final celebration
would never take place – unless, of course, the long preparations
might themselves be considered a festival. Radiswill strongly
cautions against this tempting but simplistic interpretation.
Granted, he says, the weeks of labor sustained a festive spirit,
joining all members in a common social ritual, and yet the solemn
conclusion defeats the premise of a celebration and deliberately
undercuts the higher purpose of the tribe's work. In so doing, the
end of the preparations subtly mimes the sacrificial logic of the
potlatch while bending at the same time to the reigning logic of
thrift and economy. This is no "hybrid rite" of modern tribal life,
Radiswill argues, but rather an act of stubborn dissidence. He
rejects in advance any claims that would see in the aborted
festival the syncretic "bricolage" of a mutating tribal tradition
caught in a cross-cultural postcolonial predicament. Rather, the
tribes invented something entirely new in their festival: an
authentic ritual form paradoxically lived in the mode of irony.
Here Radiswill picks up a thread first suggested in Coombes'
"Mickey Mouse." "Social practices," the anthropologist argues,
"are not so much passed on 'unknowingly', as sociologists are
ready to assert, but *unbelievingly*, in bad faith yet without cynical
bile. Culture is *camp*." (107).

The evidence on which Radiswill bases his claims may appear
fairly scant. Indeed, his reconstruction of the tribal festival
derives solely from the cassette found in Coombes' office, a
recording of Glenn Gould's famous *Goldberg Variations*. A native
informant's voice can be heard intruding at times on the music,
which is itself marked in places by the pianist's own notorious
humming and groaning. The single unidentified voice, likely that
of a Tsimshian woman, seems to refer to the new festival, but
only elliptically and in passing. Radiswill transcribes the
following testimony:

We were all sorry to say goodbye to the costumes and masks. But it was pride that made us do it. At least they wouldn't end up in your museums. Anyway, a young girl learns a lot from unweaving. When she is older she might be the seamstress, and her own daughter put back the thread. Or at least she keeps the memory of the fabric she held in her hands as she pulled it to shreds (145).

Elsewhere, the voice continues, "Those preparations were the happiest times in my life. It was like a dream. There were always some who questioned, saying, 'why?' But it's not the end that gives meaning to what we do. Life is preparation for nothing" (162).

Radiswill names his anonymous native informant "the Tsimshian Penelope," evoking the classic figure of Odysseus' wife. As Homer relates, Penelope staved off her importunate suitors for years by weaving a funeral shroud for her father only to secretly unweave it during the night. In this way Penelope managed to stay true to her absent husband, and her faithfulness took the form of an act of piety toward a family elder. Similarly, the Tsimshian Penelope is a dutiful wife and daughter; her work is a patient act of defiance and a foil to outside aggressors and their invading culture. Like the more extravagant excesses of the potlatch, moreover, her work is seemingly useless, but is in fact a deliberate bid for survival.

Years of inquiries by Radiswill among the First Nations have turned up no corroboration of his findings. He concludes that the bands remain sworn to secrecy, though the festival itself seems to have been abandoned for many years, perhaps decades. The reader of *Masks of the Ceremony* is left with a stirring ethnographic account that, however persuasive, flirts nonetheless with a sense of fabrication, as when Radiswill speculates that the Tsimshian woman's phrase, "It was like a dream" implies that the festival aspired to the state of figments conjured by the sleeping mind and erased at daybreak. "Stories composed but never told," Radiswill says, "choreography without dancers, music without voices, and who knows what other marvelous creations conceived then aborted" (183). Underscoring the last term, Radiswill speculates that the festival may even have involved the ultimate ritual sacrifice – a possibility he entertains only so far but that he is unwilling to exclude.

What, then, of Coombes' *Mask*, that paltry contribution to the field of anthropology? Radiswill claims for Coombes a role similar to that of the Tsimshian Penelope. *Mask*, Radiswill asserts, aimed at nothing more than the bare requirements for tenure and implicitly presents itself as an exercise in wasted time. With his position secured at Simon Fraser University, Coombes became academic dead wood, a seeming dilettante and amateur collector of native paintings, carvings and artifacts. But for years Coombes must have lent his support to the tribes' covert ceremonies, about which he was sworn to secrecy. As Coombes himself said, "a mask does not hide, it shows. But it shows what cannot be revealed" (231).

244 pp.

Jan Tinsman, *A Secret Life*

In her book *The Art of Memory* Frances Yates resurrected a system of memorization once lost in antiquity. According to the "method of loci" one recollects something, such as a speech or a poem, by stringing out its elements along a familiar space evoked by the mind. One makes an alibi before the judge while walking down the hallway of one's childhood home; one recites a poem to one's lover while dusting the china in a familiar cabinet. I am here, but I am also there, and this bond between disparate places and times assures my presence of mind in the current task. The artifice of this technique is what strikes us, not its affinity with the ordinary life of the mind. When, after all, am I not occupied with some scrap of memory while doing a mundane errand? Imagine, however, that it were not a text one needed to recall but instead the present itself; imagine that the life you were living now were itself a script called up by the work of another self roaming your familiar haunts. And what if that other self wandered off to tend to his own affairs? This is the apparently deluded theory Jan Tinsman develops to explain his life and mental troubles in *A Secret Life*.

Diagnosed with schizophrenia at the age of 23 and later interned in a psychiatric hospital, Tinsman began this "double autobiography" as a journal to help in his therapeutic treatment. At the time Tinsman was tormented by the thought that there existed another version of his self in the world, who unlike him was leading a healthy, productive life. Moreover, the life of that other self was continually present to his mind as if by telepathy, haunting the familiar sites of Tinsman's childhood. At the age of 36, though, Tinsman's symptoms disappeared and his doctors declared him cured. It is at this time that Tinsman began working on the manuscript for *A Secret Life*. As Tinsman explains it, his "companion," as he calls him, eventually developed the symptoms of Tinsman's former ailment, leaving Tinsman of sound mind. This folds into his narrative an odd paradox, however: apparently cured by the transfer of his illness, Tinsman nonetheless holds onto what seems a delusional fantasm. His cure, in other words, is based on a figment that itself suggests a schizophrenic state.

A Secret Life is a remarkable testament to the power and pitfalls of memory. Tinsman traces the origin of his strange theory of a remembered present to the phrase his mother used when referring to his early bouts of madness; "you're forgetting yourself," she would tell the boy (27). In this way, the mother's gentle chiding, in words that seem carefully chosen to avoid a stricter diagnostic language, instead lays the seeds for the author's lifelong delusion. When a copy of *The Art of Memory* falls into Tinsman's hands the author develops a full account of his mental condition. This account is a narrative – but also perhaps a fiction, a literary means for the author to rid himself of a demon. Indeed, much of Tinsman's therapy was in fact devoted to the supernatural novels and stories he read while interned, and in which he sought examples of the troubles plaguing him. Oddly enough, his sessions with the doctor resemble exercises in literary criticism, rather than a clinical treatment; there are discussions of Byron, E.T.A. Hoffmann, Maupassant, Bierce and Conrad, among others (34-9; 44; 51-62). With the aid of this literature, Tinsman may well have learned to see through his delusions, as his doctor seems to have believed. More troubling, though, is the prospect that Tinsman may have fabricated his own cure, that the healthy life he recounts toward the end of *My Secret Life* is the life of a character he has assumed as his own.

By the time he is a teenager, Tinsman's family has moved house many times, and in what seems a case of ordinary nostalgia Tinsman carries with him distinct memories of all these places he had lived in the past. These places are not, however, willingly called up as memories, but instead resemble a continuous film projected in his mind and accompanying his every moment in the present. Tinsman comes to believe that his "companion" lives in his childhood neighborhood, and it is through his eyes that he sees that neighborhood; later, the "companion" is living in the Charleston of his early teenage years. In a particularly striking scene, the "companion" is walking the lanes of Charleston while Tinsman is having his first sexual encounter. This double optic creates a narrative that is always rent in two, yet with a strange poetic beauty, as when he describes the naked body of his girlfriend "read" and "recalled" by his fingers like a landscape at once familiar and strange (109). Apparently, as in Yates' memory technique, Tinsman's lovemaking is dictated by that silent "companion" elsewhere. This scene is the trigger of a descent into paranoia, during which Tinsman becomes convinced he is the puppet of his other self. His panic increases as the "companion" moves closer to the places of Tinsman's current life; the life of the "companion" is catching up with Tinsman's own existence. What ensues, however, is not a monstrous encounter, but only the merging of the two, which happens while Tinsman is sedated and confined to his bed. Tinsman is eventually cured when the "companion," now mad himself, separates off to live a life that the author still follows in his mind.

The plot of *A Secret Life* has the shape of an hourglass, or perhaps the X of a chiasmus; two life paths cross ways at the center, where inverted yet parallel figures meet and diverge. As a result, the strangest moments in Tinsman's book are not those in which he narrates his delusional states or the secret life of his other self, but rather those at the center of the hourglass, where he merges, or nearly so, with his "companion." Waking from his long anguish, Tinsman feels the close presence of the "companion," who is soon to take his leave.

Writing these lines, I'm aware of a voice in my mind, lagging behind like a stubborn kid, murmuring, "Writing these lines, I'm aware of a voice in my mind, lagging behind…" No escape from this voice-over. In the same way, brushing my teeth and combing my hair, I'm aware of myself doing the same thing, brushing my teeth, combing my hair. And looking up at the mirror I do not see myself but only a face looking this way, at the site of an eclipse. And yet I am feeling better. So whose mind is it, wandering now, a field, a downward slope, a hollow, I know this place, to lie down and forget would be bliss, among the weeds, their damp roots like sod-choked lungs… (168).

Passages like these remain with the reader of *A Secret Life*, for they convey the lucidity of a consciousness that, though not fully mad, is nonetheless starkly riven. One is left with the haunting sense of an ordinary ailment that splits us from ourselves when doing two things at once, whether in a flight of the imagination, when revisiting a distant memory, or just looking out the window chewing gum.

341 pp.

Howard Loomis, *Legends of Memory*

A familiar book can sometimes call up memories of where you first read it: a former home, a vacation retreat, or a sequence in space – train trip, hotel room, distant cities – where you traveled with the book in hand. At other times you might faintly recall the thoughts accompanying that reading: the daydreams and scattered impressions that shadowed the words on the page. More faintly still, you may sense the memories that occupied your mind at the time. In such cases, you are dimly remembering the memories that accompanied your prior reading, like boxes nested in boxes. The trigger for these recollections is more visceral than an image; it is a "legend," as Howard Loomis has it, an index as strong yet as impalpable as perfume on the skin. The book in your hands is a portal to these memories; an entire world of the past opens up beyond the printed page.

Just as a book may call up the reader's memories, it also bears the traces of its author's latent thoughts and impressions. The topics of Loomis' book are "legends" of this kind that guide one's thoughts to the periphery of conscious memory. Loomis borrows his term not from myth or history, but rather from the language of cartography, and unlike other literary critics, he refers less to narrative, rhetoric and style than to "scales," "elevations," "triangulations," and "ley lines." This cartographic method aims to map a deeper layer of memories and unconscious impressions that sketch out a space larger than the text and its apparent subjects, evoking "the season and the territory, the *air du temps,* but also the furniture and the things at hand: a thimble, a goldfish in the bowl, or it is two? Look closer..." (39).

A distinguished Proust scholar, Loomis is clearly influenced by the French novelist's theory of remembrance and his vision of a past resurrected by the nearly magical power of involuntary recollection. While building on this model, Loomis' work is strikingly original, however. Loomis' cartographic method holds that a text contains the map of its larger context and that the work of the critic is to establish the links and legends charting the way to that map. Since Proust's memories are always filtered through his own thoughts and sensations, this restricts the author's theory of recollection, Loomis says. Proust's text evokes other memories, however, of which the author is unaware. When the writer's elbow rests on the table, it connects to that piece of furniture, to the floor, to the house and to the world beyond. Likewise, his words are linked to his world like objects in space; they are not "symbols," Loomis says, but things bound to other things, "in spatial propinquity, like secret companions walking arm in arm" (104).

The critic takes great pains to argue that his approach involves more than merely situating a book in its historical context; it is simple enough, for instance, to spell out the effects of political exile on the work of Victor Hugo. More to the point, Loomis says, are the traces of Hauteville House that may be found in the books Hugo wrote there. The island light, the Guernsey heath, the views from the house can be shown to permeate even the urban scenes of *Les Misérables.* And yet to make such links is still to chart mere "constellations" of the map in question.

A reader may pride himself on discovering new constellations sparkling in the text. What he has done, however, is merely connect the dots. The stars are not pebbles scattered in a void; they glint in a field of stars as thick as sand on a beach. We must imagine such an expanse of grains and add to it an unfathomable depth to conceive the true chart of the text (24).

Loomis puts his method to the test in his chapter on Proust, focusing in particular on the passages about the Vinteuil sonata and the modest "little phrase" of music that awakens in Proust a sense of the permanence of memory. Loomis musters all of his expertise to gloss these passages of Proust, considered by many the most searching and complex literary meditations on the work of anamnesis. However, Loomis has his sights on a text that lies beneath Proust's own, and the *Remembrance* seemingly fades like a sheet of tracing paper as the scholar hunts the chart lying beneath it. For Loomis, the famous Vinteuil phrase is a distraction from this quest, buzzing like a fly in his ear, as he says, or worse, pestering him "like the jingle of an ice-cream cart making its rounds" (178). Remarkable in a Proust scholar, Loomis voices impatience with what he calls the author's "prattle" as he listens instead to "a deeper murmur, the hum of voices and music nearly drowned out by Proust's grandiloquence" (184).

Over thirty years in the making, Loomis' book was his sole research while Professor of Romance Languages at Williams College and the manuscript remained incomplete when he was urged into retirement. His students often complained of his teaching style, which consisted entirely of lectures, during which he would gloss literary passages, breaking into imaginary dialogues, sometimes in falsetto, or launching into snippets of songs and ditties. One student's judgment was typical: "I felt he was reading a different text than what was assigned." Based on his cartographic analysis, Loomis claimed to know what Joyce had eaten the day he penned the final lines of "The Dead," a claim one critic dismissed as "preposterous – and irrelevant into the bargain." His commentaries of poems, judged unpublishable, were as convoluted and nearly as lengthy as Joyce's late works.

The scholar's last years were spent in New York where, to be near the haunts of Henry James, he took an apartment just off Washington Square, but he died of a pulmonary infarction before completing *Legends of Memory*. Loomis' final and unfinished chapter was occupied with James' ghost stories, focusing notably on "The Jolly Corner" and "The Great Good Place." The two stories deal with supernatural alter-egos; in "The Jolly Corner" the character is a baleful figment of James' former self, and in "The Great Good Place" it is a seemingly benevolent "brother" who shares something, however, with a haunting specter. A ghostwriter in James' employ, this spectral presence completes James' work while he is sleeping; when the author awakes he is glad to see at his desk the always turned back of his "brother" steadily working away.

In the postscript to Loomis' book, his editor makes a stunning conjecture about the author's final chapter and his death. Notes and drafts Loomis left behind suggest that the scholar was trying to uncover another character hidden beneath James' disturbing tales. These drafts are disorganized, though, and contain, along with his commentaries, detailed descriptions of Loomis' own New York life, floor plans of his apartment, and maps of his daily itineraries. Plans for the book seem to trail off into a scrapbook, and readers of Loomis' manuscript speculated that the critic may have abandoned his research to begin composing an autobiography. His editor came to another conclusion, however. The scholar's "journal," he claims, is in fact the dictation of clues he uncovered in James' stories. Loomis, in other words, would have discovered the character hidden in James' tales: the figure of a future researcher, a posthumous inheritor of James, who Loomis recognized, probably too late, as the figure of his own self already contained in the texts he was reading.

383 pp.

Alice Mei Chen, *The Beaten Track*

In this remarkable work of Alice Chen, a young Chinese-American poet, the author draws on Hemingway's *Green Hills of Africa* to compose lyric poems of subtle power and wry reflexive wit. The poet's highly unusual gambit involves an ingenious reworking of the physical text of Hemingway's safari narrative. Chen's book is the identical size and format as a 1970s' edition of Hemingway's book and shares the same cover art. Inside, Chen has crafted her poems from Hemingway's own words; these words, moreover, appear in the same place on Chen's page as they do in the source book, as if cut out from the text, leaving the remaining pages largely blank. The result is a set of poems whose verses lie scattered across the pages in a manner evocative of Mallarmé's *Un coup de dés*.

The Beaten Track is a striking demonstration that writing, including even the personal genre of the lyric, is always composed from a common stock of words. Such is the tribute of originality, aptly captured in the title of Chen's book. Chen is not, of course, the first to explore this terrain in poetry, whose formal rigor always binds creativity to generic demands. Neither is her experimental method without precedent; one thinks, for instance, of the CoBrA group's techniques of *détournement*, in which pre-existing text was sampled, edited and subverted, of Burroughs' and Gysin's cut-ups, or Ted Berrigan's mechanical approach to composing his *Sonnets*. One would be mistaken, however, to see Chen's work as a stunt or as guided by a programmatic mission of subversion. In this regard, Chen's choice of *Green Hills of Africa* is remarkably judicious, for Hemingway's autobiographical tale is rich in the first-person singular needed for Chen's lyrical self-expression. Moreover, that "I" is more than an opportune pronoun; it is, rather, the mark of a voice of grand literary egotism that Chen wrests from the adventurer to speak in her own unassuming voice.

The linguist Roman Jakobson famously identified the function of the first-person pronoun as a "shifter." Jakobson argued that the "I" as shifter refers not to the physical self but only to the instance of speech claimed by the speaker. The "I", then, is always borrowed, belonging to no one and everyone; it cannot refer to the self as such, but only, as the linguist says, to "the person uttering 'I'". Context is all defining here, and Chen's work of poetry removes the setting from Hemingway's African safari to claim his "I" as her own. And yet, that context is not simply obliterated by Chen, but remains as the haunting subtext of Chen's own poetry. Likewise, Chen's "I" does not dispatch Hemingway but ferries his voice like a ghost into her poems. As a result, *The Beaten Track* is as much a work of original poetry as it is a commentary on the book from which it derives, as well as on the life and work of Hemingway as a whole.

This complex play of poetic self-expression and subtle commentary is displayed most compellingly in the poem Chen crafts from the scene where Hemingway narrates the tracking and shooting of an antelope. The passage is well chosen and put to marvelous use by the poet. Here it is Chen slyly tracking Hemingway, even as she speaks of a subject all her own, itself deriving from another text she invokes: an entry in her childhood diary that recounts the death of a beloved pet. The theme of Chen's animal companion thus resonates with Hemingway's hunt, implicitly challenging the heroics of the hunter and the thrill of the kill. Further, in an uncanny move, Chen makes the African hunting scene evoke a future scene, Hemingway's later suicide in Idaho, as if the encounter with the antelope already anticipated the turning of the shotgun against the author. The "I" of the poet emerges, then, from the death of the hunter already presaged in his own hunt, and perhaps, the reader suspects, even desired by a guilty Chen herself.

The role of the shifter and the borrowed "I" can be gauged in the insistent play on the word "turn" in Chen's poem. "Turn," of course, is a word rich in poetic valence that evokes the often dizzying "tropes" of figural language. "I / turn / the / page," reads one deceptively simple line, which, spaced over three pages, requires that the reader of the poem do the same. Note that at least three books are turned here at once: Chen's childhood diary, Hemingway's book, and Chen's volume of poetry. Strangely, the sense of overlapping texts is heightened by the very gesture that separates the turning pages. Later, the "turn" evokes a more ominous turning, that of the hunter's gun against himself. "Why turn this against me? / I am no longer the one who wished him dead." These lines seems to suggest the conscience of the hunter revisiting his own text, while conveying at the same time Chen's own guilt as she reflects on the death of her dog. The poem finally ends, "We say the dead turn away. / But I turned first and I turn still." One hesitates to say, though the temptation is too great, that Hemingway must be turning in his grave. But the pun is perhaps in the spirit of Chen's book, which mixes a keen critical sensibility and poetic craft with playfulness and disarming wit.

No doubt Chen's feminine perspective also inspired her choice of Hemingway for *The Beaten Track*. Hemingway is a notoriously masculinist writer, and his book is larded with awkward features, including the repeated reference to his wife as "Poor Old Mama," abbreviated, lamely enough, as "P.O.M." in the text. Any glance at *Green Hills of Africa* notes these three letters that stud the entire text like a monogram, drawing attention to a person the narrative grants only a minor role. In poems that are strangely faithful to the original even in their bold adaptations, the only liberty Chen takes with Hemingway's book is to change these letters to read "P.O.E.M." Chen makes good use of this in a poem that conveys the awakening of poetic insight in the mind of a child, or possibly a mentally handicapped person. Like a voice in limbo or straining to give birth to itself, it grasps at a higher language it claims in snatches only to revert to a state of torpor.

"P.O.E.M." is the inarticulate name for the verses the voice intuits in this state of anguish and yearning. Further, the voice in "P.O.E.M" might well be that of Hemingway himself, as imagined by Chen, struggling to emerge as poet from his all-too masterful prose. In this way, Hemingway's crude nickname does not serve his condescension but instead the humble work of poetic creation lying dormant in his book.

The reader of *The Beaten Track* may wish to have Hemingway's original text at hand to best appreciate the perspicacity of Chen's work of creative citation. And since the words of her poems are scattered widely across the pages, one might read them with pen in hand, transcribing them in more legible form.

245 pp.

Arno Zweig, *Dead Ends*

There is a children's game that can develop into a kind of neurosis. "Step on a crack, break your mother's back," goes the refrain, as kids skip over crevices on the playground and sidewalk. One sometimes sees a swerve or a fitful step in adults too, suggesting the innocent game has left behind a hobbling superstition. The author of *Dead Ends* has a similar obsession, also deriving from his childhood: faced with any fork in his path, he is paralyzed by the thought of the route he will choose not to take. That route, moreover, is not simply an alternative rejected, an abandoned choice, a false option; it is a *dead end*, the terminal point of a life pursued that far and no further. *Dead Ends* is Zweig's autobiography of these aborted lives, sensed at the many crossroads that have confronted him from youth through adulthood. Zweig's crossroads include many forks in the road, but also the option of elevator or stairs, or the choice of this or that door, including, oddly enough, even "men" and "women."

Like cracks on the sidewalk, the crossroad seems to bar the way at Zweig's every step, and at such places, he says, "I feel one thread of my life peel away, as from a thick braid of possibilities. So of course I pause to measure that thread. It leads no further, but only back into the braid of my other lives" (29).

Dead Ends opens, appropriately enough, with an exergue from Dante, the first words of *The Divine Comedy*: "midway along the journey of our life / I found myself in a dark wood..." (1). Zweig's quote signals that his book is in familiar territory: his autobiography takes on the time-honored topics of freedom and choice, as well as the regrets, errors and nostalgia that may confront anyone at a crossroads. In Zweig's hands, though, these topics yield no fruitful choice, no redemption or solace. Zweig's "midway," unlike Dante's, is not so much a point of departure as a place where he stands frozen before another dreaded decision. One is accustomed to the idea that many options open up before the choices we make in life. Zweig, however, like an existentialist in reverse, sees his past as a weave of multiple lives that keep coming to an end. How does one relate the story of these "other lives"? How tell the story of a life that seems to be perpetually ending and leading constantly back?

Zweig's book makes for challenging reading, since it does not progress as narrative tends to do, in a sequence of acts and consequences, but only in fits and starts, and by retracing steps from every dead end. Virtual lives are reconstructed from Zweig's merest inclinations, passing fancies and daydreams, and in this way the book fosters a vision of life as a sum of innumerable possibilities, even if it does so in a saturnine and increasingly tragic mode. Toward the end of the text, as a desperate Zweig tries to "knot the braid" of his lives, the author is almost completely paralyzed. "Not to choose, look neither left nor right. A crack on the wall dead ahead. Not to look. No – not to choose looking or not looking. I am at the end of my rope, but no matter, pick up a thread, follow it back..." (279).

A dark wood indeed. Echoes of Dante's "midway journey" appear early on in Zweig's book when he tells of a high school class in which the students read two perennial staples of school anthologies: a pair of poems by Robert Frost. In the first poem, the line "Two roads diverged in a yellow wood" grips the young Zweig in a panic fear. Frost's poem, as is well known, relates the poet's choice of the less-traveled leafy path and his momentary pause as he considers the route not taken. What sticks with the horrified Zweig, though, is the poem's pregnant pause and the sense of a mistake never to be corrected. The other poem of Frost's describes the poet stopping in snowy woods; here there is no choice of paths, only the impatience of the horse at the poet's delay. In Zweig's mind, however, the two wan elegies merge to elaborate a nightmare. Indeed, Zweig comes to believe that the two poems are versions of a secret poem never penned by Frost.

Zweig's poetic insight leads to speculations as outlandish as they are compelling. As reconstructed by Zweig, this secret text would have combined the features of both Frost poems, the choice of paths in the leafy woods, and the pause in the snow. This "true" poem would have come before the choice between the two poems known to us, and each of those poems would be, in a sense, a betrayal of the murdered original. In that *urtext*, a literally frozen Frost would have been unable to choose his path, dying undecided in the gloom of the snowy woods. Zweig uses only Frost's own words to reconstruct the missing poem. "Oh, stopping here is a mistake / Between the woods and frozen lake / I doubt if I should travel both / One will not see me in the undergrowth" (42). Unknowingly, then, Frost would have reached a dead end, and the extant poems are merely deceptions that cover up the death of one of his life's threads. "School crams these poems down our throats," Zweig bitterly concludes, "making us believe we can easily choose between pausing and going or between two paths in the woods. But someone died there in the snow" (44).

This might seem the construct of a morbid personality, and the reader may not be persuaded by Zweig's poetic reconstruction any more than he is of Zweig's other lives. But as a reader, so to speak, of his own existence, Zweig composes alternate lives that rarely seem outright fiction, but instead hover "midway" between the plausible and the implausible, between invention and recollection.

293 pp.

Philip Kerbord, *Orinocos of the Heart*

In 1951, a team of Franco-Venezuelan geographers charted the source of the Orinoco, claiming one of the last great prizes in modern exploration. Thirty years later, a Canadian man found reason to doubt the results of the Orinoco survey. With the help of satellite imaging Philip Kerbord located a different source for the Orinoco and made a solo journey into the Venezuelan highlands to prove his claim, but after five grueling months in the upper watershed he could only confirm the findings of the 1951 expedition. It seemed Kerbord had done nothing but repeat that earlier journey until he made an unexpected discovery about a missing member of its crew. Kerbord's narrative, *Orinocos of the Heart*, takes the reader on a quest into an unsolved mystery that hinges on a notorious literary hoax.

Among the team of specialists on the 1951 expedition was a young Frenchman with no training in the field, hired as secretary-archivist of the mission. The "poet," as his colleagues called him, had recently graduated with a degree in literature from the Sorbonne. Once in Caracas the young man was overcome by the tropical climate and at the hospital he was diagnosed with a life-threatening heart ailment, a severe mitral-valve prolapse. The condition is congenital, and since his own father had died at the age of 42, André Alain learned he was facing a premature death that, his doctors assured him, would only be hastened by the demands of jungle exploration. Alain promptly resigned from the team and booked a return boat to Paris, bidding his colleagues goodbye in a letter that ended with a poetic flourish: "*Bonne route, mes amis.* As for me, I will explore the Orinocos of the heart." Upon his release from the hospital in Caracas Alain disappeared and was never heard from again. Based on his own findings Kerbord believes Alain made his way alone up the Orinoco, ending up in the region of the Casiquiare river.

Alain's life after his disappearance is linked to the Casiquiare's unique features, Kerbord claims. The river is a geographical anomaly; at a bend on the Upper Orinoco it splits off from the current, defying the rule of confluence to follow a different course. Such "distributaries," as they are called, are common enough in deltas, where multiple channels may branch out from a river. The Casiquiare, however, is not found in a wending delta network; it is a large, swiftly-flowing river. Moreover, it does not rejoin the Orinoco but turns to follow a reverse course. A naturally-occurring canal, the Casiquiare leaves the Orinoco watershed to feed instead into the Amazon basin, reaching the Atlantic more than a thousand miles from the Orinoco's Caribbean delta. The French have a special claim on the Casiquiare, since La Condamine's exploration of the region in 1743 confirmed its long-rumored and much-doubted existence. Alain's connection to the Casiquiare may owe something to this French legacy of exploration, but his own reasons for traveling there were deeply personal, Kerbord surmised. Alain would have found in the Casiquiare a symbolic emblem of his own fatal ailment, since the anomalous bifurcation of the Orinoco is akin to the young man's valvular disorder. In both cases, flow is diverted from its normal course, threatening the main current. How does a river survive such a curious ailment? What if the Orinoco were to leave its bed and follow the Casiquiare, becoming a mere tributary of the Amazon? Alain apparently sought answers to these questions as he pursued the implications of his malady. As Kerbord says,

A river is often invoked as a potent symbol of life and fatality. It tends always and only downward on a path uniquely its own. Starting out young and brisk, it grows sluggish with age; a meandering river near its finish is called "senile." And though its death is bitter when it merges with the briny sea, that end always invokes the promise of an afterlife. The Orinoco, however, defies the fates; it lives two separate lives and pursues two different goals. It symbolizes not the faint hopes of the hereafter but a life that can diverge, change course. Another life – not as a vain promise, but as a lived alternative. After receiving his death sentence Alain went on a quest for the secret of this other life (61).

Kerbord's hypothesis dawned on him as he descended the Orinoco after his failed quest in the headwaters. The dense green banks of the river were broken more and more often by open tracts of pasture, farmland and the garish patchwork of fishing villages. Kids smacked the water and called out as his craft lazed by on a barely-rippling surface filled with popcorn clouds. The landscape was close, flat and horizonless, but Kerbord sensed the approach of a line as sharp as a cliff and the pull of Amazonia like a lopsided gravitational force. At the mouth of the Casiquiare he stopped at a Jesuit mission where he learned of the curious visit of a Frenchman some thirty years earlier. The Frenchman did not give his name, saying only that he was on a "spiritual hunt." The Jesuits granted him lodging for several months, during which time the young man worked in the mission library, barely speaking with the resident monks. He finally departed without notice, leaving behind the memory of a feverish and introspective stranger given at times to saintly raptures. Kerbord identified this Frenchman as none other than the "poet" from the 1951 expedition. He resolved to piece together the story of Alain's life and learn the purpose of his quest on the Orinoco.

As Kerbord recounts, the Jesuits were struck by the fact that Alain consulted no religious texts in the library, only literary works, and though they did not keep records of his reading the library director was able to show Kerbord the shelves he had consulted, which included a haphazard collection of French poetry. Alain begged the mission to order current literary journals and magazines from France, and the director vividly remembered his agony at the delay in receiving them. Every day, he said, the boy could be seen trudging off to meet a mail boat that seldom pulled into dock. The monks put Alain's remaining affairs into storage after he left, and poring over the contents of the box Kerbord noted that one story predominated in the Parisian literary press of the day: the excitement and scandal following the publication of Arthur Rimbaud's "The Spiritual Hunt" in 1949. The title of Rimbaud's poem immediately struck Kerbord, since it was the same phrase Alain had used to explain his presence in the Casiquiare. It seemed the "poet" had been on a literary quest.

With a telegraph at his disposal Kerbord was able to confirm his intuition by contacting Alain's surviving family. Like Alain, though, Kerbord had to endure long delays waiting for documents he requested, but he profited from his time at the mission by starting work on the manuscript that would become *Orinocos of the Heart*. Kerbord learned that when Alain embarked on the Orinoco expedition he had recently completed a dissertation on Rimbaud's visionary poems, focusing on his "Drunken Boat," as well as on the recently-discovered "Spiritual Hunt." The publication of this long-lost manuscript of Rimbaud's seemed to be a boon to the ambitious young student; appearing as it did while he was drafting his study, Alain was well placed to make a timely intervention in a major scholarly debate. What Alain didn't know at the time he boarded the boat to Venezuela, however, is that "The Spiritual Hunt" was in fact a hoax. And in a perverse twist of fate, the unveiling of the fraud occurred while Alain was en route and out of contact with the news.

Here Kerbord's book takes an unexpected but rewarding foray into French literary history. "The Spiritual Hunt" is no doubt one of the world's great literary hoaxes. Verlaine and Rimbaud's correspondence refers to a manuscript with that title, purportedly lost along with a collection of private letters when the two poets fled to England after the exposure of their homosexual relationship. Verlaine called the poem Rimbaud's "masterpiece," and critics have long speculated on its possible treasures. However, given the conflict with Verlaine's wife, who was pursuing a divorce, others believe the existence of the manuscript was contrived by the poets as a ploy to reclaim compromising papers. The unexpected "discovery" of the poem in 1949 set off a firestorm in the literary community. André Breton was quick to denounce it as a fake, though other prominent figures, including Jean Paulhan, spoke to its authenticity. Alain's dissertation shows he was clearly among the believers. The true authors of "The Spiritual Hunt" finally came forward to admit to their deception in July 1949.

By departing France in late June of that year Alain was sacrificing an opportunity – ill-fated, in retrospect – to join the literary discussion about "The Spiritual Hunt." On the other hand, though, his joining of the expedition fulfilled a dream inspired by the visionary poet. Rimbaud, after all, is the writer who famously traded in his pen for a life of adventure, disappearing at a young age into the wilds of Abyssinia. Before his departure for Africa, Rimbaud's vision of discovery and adventure was captured in the fierce and magical opening lines of his "Drunken Boat."

As I was floating down unconcerned Rivers
I no longer felt myself steered by the haulers:
Gaudy Redskins had taken them for targets
Nailing them naked to coloured stakes.

As Kerbord points out, Rimbaud's reference to "Redskins" clearly places this opening stanza in the Americas, and perhaps on the Orinoco itself. But the link to the Orinoco is made even more insistent by the poem's second stanza.

I cared nothing for all my crews,
Carrying Flemish wheat or English cottons.
When, along with my haulers those uproars were done with
The Rivers let me sail downstream where I pleased.

The word "Rivers" in the first and eighth verses is oddly ungrammatical, as Kerbord notes, and yet the poet employs it in both stanzas. *Fleuve*, Rimbaud's choice of noun, refers generally to rivers that end at the sea, and not to tributaries; *rivière* is the more encompassing term in French. Rimbaud's plural *fleuves* would be a contradiction in terms were it not for the Orinoco, unique among rivers for dividing and spilling into different seas. Only on the Orinoco could the drunken boat entertain the paradoxical journey the word implies, taking two trips to the ocean in one go. Kerbord now saw that the boat's aimless trip downstream subtly hides a willful decision on the poet's part: the choice of a duplicitous twinned journey that anticipates the marvels awaiting the boat on its wild ocean adventure. Indeed, as Kerbord argues, those marvels are only possible thanks to the fantastical premise of the boat's "double journey," as he puts it (89). Though Kerbord claims no expertise in literature, his Canadian education in French serves him admirably here. It appears "The Drunken Boat" is the likely inspiration for Alain's journey, as it maps out the specific place where the exemplary poetic quest may begin. More ominously, the poem also predicts Alain's abandonment of the crew as he pursued his own course on the Orinoco. Even Alain's physical ailment is foretold by the poems he read before his departure; appropriately enough, the last two sections of "The Spiritual Hunt" are titled "Infirmities" and "Swamps."

Working in the mission library, Kerbord next sought out the source of the phrase with which Alain made his cryptic farewell to the crew: *"A moi de découvrir les Orénoques du coeur."* The phrase is a perfect French alexandrine with a classical caesura, and Kerbord suspected it was drawn from "The Spiritual Hunt" but was disappointed in his search. Undaunted, however, Kerbord then scoured every poem of Rimbaud's, and all of Verlaine, Baudelaire, Nerval, Gautier, Hugo and Mallarmé. Having exhausted Rimbaud's literary peers, Kerbord read widely in all the French literature housed at the mission, requesting further volumes from missions and monasteries in neighboring regions, as well as in French Guiana, Chile and Peru. He read Jules Verne's *The Mighty Orinoco* as well as the geographic documents on which the novelist based his tale, and updating Verne's bibliography Kerbord filled in the background to his own expedition. One of his more famous precursors, Alexander Rice, had traveled up the Casiquiare in 1924 on his way to hunt for the Orinoco's source. The explorer was accompanied by his wife Eleanor, a widowed survivor of the Titanic whose grand endowment built the Harvard library that bears her name. Kerbord was troubled by the image of Mrs Widener navigating the Casiquiare, still accompanied by the faithful maid with whom she had waited in a lifeboat while her son and first husband sank with the ship.

That night Kerbord found himself on the path to the mooring where Alain's restless comings and goings had worn a rut in the earth. He couldn't keep to the *picada* without blotting out Alain's footprints, so he advanced awkwardly, jumping back and forth over the rut as if playing hopscotch. But a hard frost covered the ground; Alain's prints were as stiff as washboards. From the shore the calm river looked like a frozen lake in winter. Kerbord recognized Mrs Widener in a long boat, outlined sharply like a paper cut-out on a landscape by the Douanier Rousseau. The gunwales were almost level with the water and Kerbord judged the boat to be just beyond the line of the horizon. Then he realized he was wrong: the boat was going to founder. He tried to call out in alarm. Mrs Widener made an imperious gesture and her companion dropped a parcel of books over the rail as if spilling a sandbag from a Montgolfière. The books bobbed at the surface, and before they sank Kerbord was amazed to see them drifting up toward the junction as if pulled by the tide (208-9).

Kerbord's stay at the mission continued to lengthen, but months of reading paid off when he finally came across the poetic line "Orinocos of the heart" buried in the prose of Baudelaire's essay "The Painter of Modern Life." Baudelaire's metaphor seemed to hint not only at the river's vast and complex jungle arteries but also at the strange hydraulics of the Casiquiare. A phrase that may have inspired Rimbaud, then Alain, finally uncovered by Kerbord, reading by lamplight in the mission library. No doubt Baudelaire's line raised questions of its own. But was there need to search any further? He remembered Ms Gieger dumping books in the river.

For Kerbord the discovery was conclusive, redeeming his failed trip to the headwaters and the worthwhile culmination of an arduous quest. Indeed, it seems the passionate hunt for one source was replaced with another as Kerbord sought the cause of Alain's Orinoco journey. Moreover, in the excitement of his research Kerbord appears unaware of an irony that will no doubt strike the reader of *Orinocos of the Heart*; pursuing the traces of the poet become adventurer, the adventurer himself turns reader of poetry – and literary critic. One imagines the studious and cloistered Kerbord almost as frenzied and rapturous as the "feverish" Alain who preceded him in the Casiquiare, and whose place Kerbord assumed in the mission library.

Bookish as it may be, Kerbord's sojourn is punctuated by a number of intriguing episodes, including a meeting with the eminent French anthropologist Pierre Clastres, conducting fieldwork among the Yanomami. Readers of Clastres' work may recognize Philip Kerbord in a veiled reference the anthropologist makes to a "Molloy in the Amazon." The cameo is fitting, coming as it does in a text that mourns the passing of the age of exploration and the end of adventure, in tones evocative of Lévi-Strauss's *Tristes Tropiques*.

Kerbord himself may not have made his mark in the annals of science, but *Orinocos of the Heart* offers discoveries and rewards of a different kind. And yet, the reader may wonder, did Kerbord truly find the reason for Alain's curious journey? Even his textual discovery seems strangely equivocal, ending as it does with plural "Orinocos." This may seem a minor quibble, though oddly enough it repeats a persistent symptom in stories of river exploration. The 1951 expedition concluded its survey not with one source of the Orinoco but rather with "two rivulets." And a hundred years earlier, in the highly-publicized search for the source of the Nile, the explorers Sir Richard Burton and John Speke had a heated disagreement over which of the two could claim the discovery as their own. The dispute came to be known as "the Nile Duel," and it ended in Speke's suspicious death, considered by many a suicide.

In Kerbord's tale of split sources, doubled journeys and wayward currents, the crowning duplicity, of course, is that of the fake "Spiritual Hunt," a text that may have decided Alain's fate. Kerbord can only speculate on Alain's life after he left the mission. No doubt he was heartbroken, Kerbord says, at learning of the hoax. Perhaps, seeking a rebirth and a reprieve from his ailment, he followed the flow of the Casiquiare toward the Amazon or joined a Brazilian tribe. He might have simply chosen the mission as a waystation, hoping to meet up with the expedition in the highlands. The author admits that the true cause of Alain's presence at the Casiquiare may never be known. The Jesuits continue to store Alain's personal effects as if believing he could return at any time.

245 pp.

John Gregory, *Crazy Quilt*

Aside from a nearly-illegible scrawl in the Creve Coeur census, the first public record of Aaron Mackay is found in the archives of the Juvenile Mental Sanitarium in Saint Louis, Missouri. Having lost his parents in the flu pandemic of 1918, the young Mackay was taken in by relatives and soon thereafter interned for "alternating bouts of high exhilaration and deep despondency" and "insistent fancies of a delusional nature." Mackay's aunt and uncle traced the first signs of the boy's ailments to his mother's funeral service; far from being depressed at the occasion, the young Mackay seemed transported by the memorial sermon and later insisted on going every following Sunday to hear the pastor speak. The boy's adoptive parents were glad he found solace in the church visits but quickly realized that his understanding of the sermons bore no resemblance to their own. The nearly hysterical boy spoke of the amazing things he had "seen" and "heard" in church and filled the week recounting extravagant stories from memory. When the pastor suddenly died Mackay insisted on being taken from one church to the next, sometimes several times a day, though he always asked to leave early, impatiently claiming that he "couldn't hear nothing no more."

Mackay spent nearly a decade at the Juvenile Sanitarium. After his release in 1929 he enrolled as a student of literature at

Washington University with ambitions of becoming a writer of fiction, but the young man was beset by depression and a crippling writer's block and had to abandon his studies in his third year. Nothing is known of his whereabouts until he resurfaced unexpectedly as the pastor of a modest new nondenominational church in East Saint Louis. From 1933 on, Mackay led a congregation that shied from all dogma and doctrines, espousing only the broadest articles of faith in the life of the spirit and the belief in the "other side."

Mackay's unassuming life would have no doubt fallen into oblivion were it not for John Gregory and his new book, *Crazy Quilt*. While on academic spring break in 1986, Gregory, a young scholar of African-American literature, accompanied his relatives to a Palm Sunday church service in East Saint Louis. A confirmed atheist, the scholar had no particular interest in the ceremonies of Holy Week, but for reasons related to his studies of literature and culture he was a willing, if abstracted, listener to the sermon that day. As chance would have it, Gregory's visit coincided with one of Mackay's final sermons in the church he had led for over fifty years. The unexpected guest at the church would make a discovery that, he contends, will forever change the landscape of modern American literature.

In his sermon that spring day the pastor did not directly address the conventional themes of Palm Sunday. Instead he spoke more generally on the theme of the "guiding spirit," often pausing between sentences, and even mid-phrase, as if listening to the echo of his words and then waiting even longer to follow their decay. At some point in the sermon the pastor spoke the following line: "If a breeze fans along and quivers the leaves it makes you feel mournful, because you feel as if it were spirits whispering – spirits that have been dead ever so many years – and you always think they are talking about *you*." Gregory instantly recognized the line – barely modified from the original vernacular – as drawn from Twain's *Huckleberry Finn*. The scholar wondered at the reason for this literary evocation in a sermon of Holy Week. Pricking up his ears to what followed, Gregory began to sense that each word of the pastor's, even the most mundane, was plucked from some enormous literary compendium and still buzzing with the muted cacophony of that hidden text. As the sermon drew to a close, the pastor made a modest reference to his long career, saying he had done nothing in all his years but guide his flock in "listening to the stillness" – another line Gregory knew came from Twain's novel.

Any bright student of American literature might have picked up on such allusions, but Gregory's career as a scholar made him especially sensitive to the textual threads woven into the pastor's sermon. In Gregory's dissertation, "'Moaning and Mourning': Black Culture in the White American Canon," the scholar argues that African-American experience is relayed in "undertones" of speech that express the "inchoate verbal matter of shared incomprehension in a checkerboard world." Gregory's own title borrows a key line from *Huckleberry Finn* that describes the plaints of the fugitive slave Jim, and the scholar parses Twain's line on "moaning and mourning" at some length to draw out the novel's "garbled undertones of racialized enunciation." Gregory argues that the critic, like a psychoanalyst, must listen with "free-floating attention" to the language around him, tuning his ear to "the other text, alive with the mutterings of the unfulfilled and the inarticulate vanities of the master." An obsessive figure in Gregory's dissertation is the "sub-text": a layer below the surface, sometimes called a "lining" or the "underside," invisible yet audibly awakened to the ear that listens in. Accordingly, in his graduate studies at Howard University Gregory was an avid lecture-goer, though he increasingly gravitated toward talks outside his field of study so as not to be distracted from those deeper murmurings. He became a regular fixture at lectures in business administration and constitutional law, and eventually even Earth sciences and astronomy, jotting notes with no direct bearing on the lectures' ostensible topics. It was with just such dreamlike inattention that Gregory sat down in the pew to take in Mackay's service, all the while musing on the arcana of his own dissertation, which, following his visit to Saint Louis, he would soon abandon in order to write *Crazy Quilt*.

Leaving the church that day and caught up in a "sustained reverie" (24), Gregory meditated on familiar scenes from Twain's book. One passage insistently came back to him: an episode of languorous repose at daybreak, when Huck and Jim, sleeping, waking, and sleeping again, hear the sounds of "spirits" carried across the water from "the other side." It dawned on Gregory that the familiar scene came to him not from his own memory but was instead dictated by words scattered across the pastor's sermon and affecting him at a remove, like sparks falling from the steamship whose wake reaches Jim and Huck long after it has passed them by. The pastor's sermon had embroidered on the theme of the divine message and focused especially on John the Baptist, the holy "messenger" ministering on the banks of the Jordan, whose life, ending with his beheading, foretold the miracles of the one who walked "over the water." Underlying the pastor's sermon, it seemed to Gregory, were the following lines from Twain: "you'd see a raft sliding by, away off yonder, and maybe a galoot on it chopping...; you'd see the ax flash and come down – you don't hear nothing; you see that ax go up again, and by the time it's above the man's head then you hear the *k'chunk!* – it had took all that time to come over the water" (31). Gregory's hair tingled at the back of his neck. The pastor had apparently glossed Twain's episode as an allegory of John's martyrdom and the coming of the divine word. Strange and ingenious as this was, Gregory sensed that yet another text lay in hiding beyond the sermon, whose belated message he could only barely make out.

When Gregory returned to the church the following week, the old white pastor was replaced by a charismatic young black preacher and the congregation filled every seat. As Gregory learned, the old pastor had been approached in the past year by the young preacher, who, looking to increase his flock, suggested a merging of the two congregations, with an alternating schedule of ministrations. The old pastor was assured a better livelihood with this arrangement, as his own congregation had dwindled to a mere two dozen souls in recent years. Built in the early twentieth century, the pastor's church had once served a white working-class neighborhood but now found itself squarely in a black ghetto. His parishioners were mostly poor white folks from the nearby retirement home, though a few faithful families still drove in on Sundays from further afield. The young preacher may well have bet on what would result from the deal he struck with the old pastor: the white folks mostly stayed away on alternating weeks and those who remained, visibly uncomfortable among the new black crowd, dwindled quickly in numbers, while the black congregation, respectful at first, soon showed impatience with the old pastor's rambling orations. The new flock was treated every other week to a sermon of disjointed halting phrases, in which the pastor accented seemingly random words, and occasionally the name of a saint, after which he would pause as if to allow the listener time to revisit a private hagiography. At other times he would fall into complete silence for minutes on end, causing many to think he had lost his train of thought. Each sermon picked up a perpetual theme, that of the "other side," apparently an invocation of the spiritual beyond, though Gregory had begun to intuit a different meaning to the words. Mackay's silent pauses, he surmised, were a key to that "other side," though in the new church those silences were broken more and more with coughs, whispers, and uncomfortable shufflings, distracting to Gregory but to which the pastor himself paid no mind.

At the risk of dismissal from his adjunct teaching position at a community college, Gregory stayed on in Saint Louis to hear the old pastor's last sermons. By this time the scholar had developed a hypothesis about the sermons, though incredulity still kept him from directly approaching the pastor. His suspicions were confirmed, however, on the final Sunday, when the pastor began his sermon with a line unmistakably drawn from the beginning of Nabokov's *Speak, Memory*. "Our existence," Mackay intoned, "is but a brief crack of light between two eternities of darkness" (35). To all others in the church the passage must have seemed little more than a fairly glum homily. Gregory, however, was thunderstruck, and even more so by what followed: attuned to the reference to Nabokov, he now could tell that the remaining sermon, while never quoting from the text, in fact drew its words entirely from *Lolita*.

> To say I was stunned – *k'chunk!* – would be an understatement. Now as I recall that moment of revelation I feel spiked by a shot of adrenaline that makes it impossible to sit without moving or talk without wanting to shout! But at that moment it was just the opposite: a thrill passed through me, then passed on, like through a sieve, to the *other side*, and carrying me with it, left my body in a kind of stupor while I gazed uncomprehending at the fine, dim tracery of an infinite text or shroud unfurled in the darkness God knows where (37).

If the earlier reference to Twain might have been chalked up to Saint Louis regionalism, a holdover of adolescent fantasy, or maybe pedantic, if uninspired, hermeneutic pretensions, the invocation of *Lolita* was clearly something else: a scandalous intrusion into a religious sermon and a mystifying lure for those with open ears. Ringing throughout the sermon, insistently but as if baffled or extremely distant, was the word *quilt*, never spoken as such, yet suggested obliquely by rhymes, synonyms, and alliterations. Gregory now saw that the theme of the river was overlain with an even larger landscape: what Nabokov called the "crazy quilt" of the American continent, as *Lolita*'s fugitive narrator raced across a patchwork of roads and fields, relentlessly pursued by his nemesis. Gregory could suddenly see in his mind's eye fragments of an intricate quilt invoked by the pastor's wandering sermons: the scene of Huck and Jim on the riverbank, like a quaint folkloric image cut out from a discarded apron or kitchen towel; the murder of Clare Quilty, salvaged from *Lolita* like a scene of the passion on some disused devotional fabric. And there was more: scenes from Melville's *The Confidence-Man*; Chateaubriand's *Atala* and *René*; Twain again, and then Faulkner, Hemingway, Welty and O'Connor, among others.

Once returned to teaching, Gregory set himself the task of constructing a pattern out of these scenes pieced into the pastor's imaginary quilt. Like any good quilt, Gregory learned, it had repeating motifs: Native Americans readying for battle; ferries loading and unloading; railroads, telephone lines and Indian "traces." Increasingly, however, Gregory was perplexed by words on which the pastor had laid particular emphasis and which fit no pattern he could discern. Musing on these words he became convinced that the patchwork of familiar literary scenes was only the humble backing of a more elaborate design out of sight on the other side of the quilt. Gregory resolved to uncover at least a fragment of the other side before confronting the pastor with his discovery. A month prior to his planned return to Saint Louis, however, he learned that the pastor had been ejected from the church. The young preacher had apparently orchestrated a hostile takeover; allowing the pastor to preach long enough to convince the parishioners of his senility, he had the old man ousted on grounds of incompetence. To Gregory's frustration, the pastor had also moved out of his home and left no forwarding address. For an entire summer Gregory chased clues on Saint Louis' Skid Row, at the YMCA in Kansas City, and in Topeka, where he confirmed the sighting of an old itinerant preacher, then followed faint leads as far as Denver before the trail went cold.

This story has the makings of a narrative of its own, and indeed at times *Crazy Quilt* reads less like a scholarly exegesis than as the manuscript for an aborted work of fiction. Gregory's aims are more modest, however, and his book consists mainly of descriptions of patterns and motifs reconstructed from conversations with former church members and the interpretation of the few precious sermons recorded at memorial services and weddings. Gregory was surprised to note that on these tapes the congregation often seems to nod off to sleep, even within the first minutes of a sermon, and he had to admit the same might have happened when he was in attendance himself. As they say, a well-constructed quilt "dreams good," and Gregory found that many church members confessed to having dreams they thought were not their own, and which, moreover, resembled each other. One woman's account was especially revealing: "There's two kinds of dreams," she said. "Those you remember, and those you know you had, but can't recall." Pressing her on the point, Gregory asked her how she could know she had a dream she couldn't remember. "It comes to you in flashes," she answered. "You might be looking at a thing, say that chair, and it hits you that you had a dream about it, or as if it was hiding another chair, somehow like it, but on the other side." She gestured toward a chair, but her eye fell short of it, Gregory noticed, dropping instead onto the Toile de Jouy tablecloth between them. On the tablecloth, pastoral scenes alternated: a fiddler wooing a damsel; a young couple on a picnic blanket, children romping beyond; a farmer's wife beating clothes on a washboard; above her, sheets on the line, and a checkered tablecloth, itself decorated with pictures, perhaps. Gregory looked no closer, not wanting to make out the pickaninnies he thought must be hiding in there somewhere. There was a silence.

"What other side?" he finally asked.

"Oh, I don't know, as if everything here in this room had a double that was the same but different, and I'm sure I've been there, but I can't really say" (216-7). Helpful as it was, the old woman's testimony was basically evasive. As Gregory later learned, it was not any given object that prompted the sense of the uncanny, but rather things relating to black people; what made the church members feel they were dreaming dreams not their own was that they all had to do with a black world they didn't care to know.

The two sides of a quilt may have little in common, and if such were the case with the pastor's quilt, Gregory realized, the pieces he had so far reconstructed might provide no clue as to the pattern on what he now felt sure was Mackay's hidden masterpiece. But unlike a quilt's flat decorative pieces, the quilting stitch passes from one side of the bedding to the other; the same thread, dimpling a piece on this side, pulls the patterned fabric on the other face close to that hollow, so that the two sides nearly meet. The stitch, then, provides a key to two aspects of the quilt: its overall tactile structure, whether cursive or geometric, and the hidden design on the other side, which the thread touched each time it went out of sight. Thinking back on the words that Mackay had marked with his pregnant pauses, Gregory worked to discern a pattern to what he believed was a long, ramified quilting stitch. On the days he had heard him speak, Gregory noted the names Saint Stephen, Saint Paul and Saint George, as well as place names from holy scripture: Bethlehem, Zion, Eden, and even Utopia. It was only when taking a cab to the Saint Charles airport after a weekend's fruitless research that he suddenly realized the names the pastor had invoked were all names of places: Saint Stephen and Saint Paul, Minnesota; Saint Genevieve, Missouri and Saint George, Pennsylvania. A look at a map confirmed a Bethlehem, West Virginia, a Zion, Kentucky, a Rome, an Eden and a Utopia, Ohio. All were found on the Mississippi or its main tributaries. A host of other nouns also corresponded to places on the Mississippi, the Missouri, the Platte and the Ohio rivers: Providence,

Missouri; Trinity, Kentucky; Antiquity, West Virginia; and Freedom, Pennsylvania. These names, Gregory concluded, marked points on Mackay's quilting stitch, whose branching pattern, like the veins of an irregular leaf or a naked, twisted tree, drew the watershed of the river, stretching from Louisiana to Saskatchewan, and from Idaho to New York.

Armed with this insight, Gregory proposes "an informed conjecture" as to the pattern on the hidden face of Mackay's quilt. We leave it to the reader of *Crazy Quilt* to follow the details of Gregory's speculative reconstructions, noting here only the essentials, which, if they do not sway the skeptic, will at least persuade him of the evocative power of Gregory's work.

As he relates in his final chapter, Gregory's discovery of the quilting stitch allowed him to revisit the allusions to Twain he had heard at his first sermon and to reconsider their place in Mackay's overall pattern. When Twain first drafted *Huckleberry Finn*, the novelist had imagined tracing the journey of Huck and Jim upriver and North along the Ohio toward freedom. The plot seems to have frustrated Twain, for he abandoned the manuscript for several years, and when he later returned to the text the story had found its proper course, following the natural flow of the Mississippi southward. Interestingly, however, Twain incorporated his earlier failure into the narrative of the final text, when Huck and Jim, having lost their way in the fog, miss the confluence of the Mississippi and Ohio rivers at Cairo. For his part, Mackay, adopting Twain's organizing motif, chose instead to go in the direction of the novelist's writing block. This decision of Mackay's is, to say the least, rich in implications. It suggests that the pastor chose to make his own failed youthful ambitions as a novelist into an organizing principle of narrative. Further, Mackay's choice implicitly challenges Twain's grotesque narrative comedy of Jim's liberation. Exploding Twain's one-way southward journey, and indeed scrapping an entire canon of American writing, Mackay instead traced multiple if not infinite itineraries up every branch of the vast river system, and at each point on the quilting stitch's hidden face, Gregory argues, he embroidered the migrant stories of generations of black Americans. The piecing of these stories, moreover, followed codes employed in Underground Railroad quilts, which, hung out to air along the routes of emancipation, secretly warned and guided fugitives on the way to freedom. For Gregory this last discovery explains why Mackay would have been so willing to withdraw from his church, even under such regrettable circumstances.

The story of Underground Railroad quilts may in fact be apocryphal. Likewise, Gregory's account of Mackay's imaginary quilt will likely never yield definitive proof. Even Gregory's admirers will wonder whether the scholar has lost himself in an elaborate metaphor, such as when he attempts to divine the nature of the batting that fills the quilt, an inquiry that absorbed the scholar for near a decade (266-98). Surely, however, *Crazy Quilt* is more than willful artifice, a scholar's interpretive fantasy, or, in the words of Gregory's dissertation advisor, "a monograph, however compelling, that lacks even a modicum of verifiable data." More laconically, an early reviewer of *Crazy Quilt* proffers the cutting assessment, "Dream on," and another, no doubt meaning to be coy, but in fact merely sarcastic, asked, "To what – or whom – does the adjective in Gregory's title actually refer?" By the end of his book Gregory has clearly abandoned the illusion of an academic career, and anticipating his critics, draws on Freud to assert that "the measure of dreams is not a desirable truth but the truth of desire. Mackay shredded the dressed-up nightmares of literature and scripture and left us instead a generous patchwork on which to embroider our hopes and dreams" (307).

311 pp.

Peter Hendricks, *The Typist*

Benny O. Walter's career spanned sixty years and intersected with some of the great names of twentieth-century literature. Walter appears occasionally in histories of West Coast and Beat-era literati, but only in silhouette, as a figure somewhat ludicrous yet possessing an enigmatic power and authority. This oversight is due in part to the fact that Walter never produced any work of his own; his life was committed solely to typing the work of others. Moreover, Walter spent his last decades in anonymity and almost total seclusion, during which time he secretly embarked on an ambitious and all-consuming project to create a new manuscript of the King James Bible. Notoriously slow as a typist, Walter was only able to complete a short segment of the Old Testament before his death. He was found at his desk, emaciated, having apparently died of starvation, and surrounded ironically enough by a small fortune's worth of uterine vellum, the rare, costly and durable stationery with which he had hoped to assure his immortality.

A native of Los Angeles, in the 1930s Walter gained a reputation among friends in the movie industry for his seemingly occult talent as a typist of original screenplays. Walter was believed to have a "magic touch" as a typist; in a record that remains unmatched today, all the screenplays he put into type were optioned by film studios. None, however, advanced to production. This partial success guaranteed a livelihood for Walter and his literary friends but consigned their careers to a twilight existence. As a result, faith in the typist's magic touch gave way over time to a belief in "Benny's curse." John Fante, fellow Angeleno and early supporter of Walter's work, was one of the first to disown the typist; Fante's first published story, "Altar Boy," was sent to H.L. Mencken's *American Mercury* written in longhand, prompting Mencken's puzzled query: "Dear Mr Fante, What do you have against a typewriter?" (39).

Mencken's question is strangely prescient, for Walter's career, taking him from Los Angeles to San Francisco and New York, attests to an uncanny influence that the typist's friends and colleagues were all to disclaim. The most striking instance, no doubt, is that of William S. Burroughs. Having heard that a certain Benny Walter was writing a new version of Melville's "Billy Budd" – one of Burroughs' favorite stories – the writer was intrigued enough to set up a meeting with Walter only to learn that he was simply transcribing Melville's text verbatim. To judge from his letters, Burroughs considered the man he nicknamed "the scrivener" to be little more than a crank. Friends, however, recall that the two had many conversations about typewriters, a shared interest, as it turns out, since Burroughs was the grandson of the inventor of the adding machine and founder of the company that produced the Burroughs typewriter. And while it is well known that the Beat author embraced his role as perverse namesake of the Burroughs Corporation, Hendricks argues that his near-psychotic theories of the "soft typewriter" and "soft machine" stem directly from his encounter with the typist. Even Burroughs' sinister Doctor Benway seems to evoke the name of the enigmatic Benny Walter.

In the late 1950s, Walter began transcribing the work of Jorge Luis Borges. Among these manuscripts one text is noticeably absent, however: Borges' famous "Pierre Ménard, Author of the Quixote." In Borges' story, a modern Frenchman copies out Cervantes' masterpiece, and the narrator slyly contends that Ménard's transcription, while perfectly true to the original, is nonetheless far superior to Cervantes' text. Walter was clearly drawn to the story, whose premise seems to anticipate the typist's own career, but his encounter with Borges' "Pierre Ménard" led to no manuscript of his own. What resulted instead was a fascinating exchange of letters between the typist and the "Maestro" of the modern fable.

Walter contacted Borges in 1957 and expressed interest in

transcribing Ménard's manuscript. Would the Maestro be so good as to provide him with the text, Walter asked. Thinking perhaps that Walter was addressing him under the guise of a fictive persona, Borges gamely replied in his narrator's voice, stating that Walter might consult Cervantes' text itself, which, though falling short of Ménard's Quixote, is nonetheless identical in form. Undaunted, Walter said that he believed Ménard's text must indeed be different from the original text, adding that the typography would be of particular interest to him. Borges, now adopting the unlikely pose of a realist, conveyed with a trace of condescension that "Pierre Ménard" was, after all, "a fable." The Maestro never answered Walter's last missive, in which the typist says, "We too have been fabling, have we not? Fiction – or feint – I take Ménard's work to be no less actual on that account" (74). Did Walter mean to call Borges' bluff? Were his letters no more than a ruse? Or, as Hendricks believes, was Walter plumbing etymology to claim the distant meanings of *fable* as "conversing," and *fiction* and *feint* as "forming," "fashioning" and "fabri-cating"? Whatever the case, Walter finally sent Borges his manuscript – minus the "Ménard" – in 1958, the very year Borges succumbed to total blindness. The Maestro would apparently never read the typist's versions of his work.

Taken on their own, Hendricks' chapters on Burroughs and Borges are enough to recommend *The Typist* to any serious student of modern literature. Hendricks leaves it to future scholars, however, to gauge the extent of Walter's influence on the artists and writers of his day, for the bulk of Hendricks' book is devoted not to literary history but to an in-depth analysis of the manuscripts Walter left behind. Working with files he unearthed from Hollywood film studios, literary archives and Walter's own apartment, Hendricks makes the case that Walter's manuscripts, while apparently mere transcriptions of source-texts, are in fact subtle but far-reaching rewritings of the originals. Hendricks argues that Walter's artistry lies in his unique handiwork as a typist, a labor Walter sometimes compared to the work of typesetters of old. One of Walter's techniques, which likely passed unnoticed to his readers, was the nearly-imperceptible variation of the ¾ space that tightens the rhythm between chosen words, and the 1¼ space that subtly lengthens it. Another technique, which might readily be misattributed to faulty key-strokes, is the occasional overlap of letters, but only so much as to make them barely touch. Hard strokes, subtly highlighting letters, words and sometimes even entire passages, or, alternately, soft strokes that suggest a worn ribbon, create a constant play of tone and emphasis. None of Walter's typographical inter-polations went so far as to alter the language of the original, however. Further, Hendricks pointedly argues that the typist's modifications, however slight, should not be considered as personal improvisations on the text. Speaking of Walter's hard and soft strokes, for example, Hendricks likens them not to an actor's interpretation of a script, but to a more "impersonal" alteration akin to the slight rise and fall of volume due to sound's vagaries on the air. In one instance, drawn from Faulkner's unproduced screenplay "A Month of Rain," Hendricks claims to detect a Doppler-effect as the text recedes from the reader.

> A judicious combination of ¾ spaces, soft strokes and overlaps creates this effect, similar to the distortion of sound as its source draws away. The reader's head may not pitch forward, but an inward tropism pulls him toward the typed page. The text's murmur deepens and the key shifts; following that slight distortion, we feel a visceral nausea, as when an elevator suddenly drops beneath our feet. [...] What is it about Faulkner's innocuous phrase, "It was almost two in the afternoon," that provoked this modification on the typist's part? No suspense or foreboding is attached to the author's notation. Perhaps Walter had simply chosen this moment to underscore the message, latent here as elsewhere: *this is a text* (144).

For thirty years, from his Hollywood days to the time he finally settled in New York, Benny Walter plied his craft with his faithful Underwood. When the IBM Selectric was released in 1961, however, it instantly became Walter's machine of choice. For a typist skilled in the delicate touches Hendricks describes the IBM seems a highly unlikely medium. After all, its electric motor and rotating typeball mechanism would appear to preclude any variation in stroke on the typist's part. And yet it is on this machine, the epitome of speed, convenience and standardization, that Walter composed his most significant work.

Beginning in 1961, Walter set himself the task of composing new manuscripts of Blake, Wordsworth, Eliot, James, Kafka and Conrad. The case of the latter is especially intriguing, for, as Hendricks argues, Walter's Conrad manuscripts bring to light an author quite unlike the one known from his extant books. Conrad's adopted English often betrays an odd syntax inherited from his native Polish and his vocabulary is studded with frequent borrowings from French. In Walter's manuscripts, however, the novelist's linguistic complexity approaches the heteroglossia of the later Joyce. As a result, Walter's Conrad is not as he is generally thought a mere precursor of Modernism but its first and possibly greatest exponent. The author's tone, sometimes bombastic and stentorian in his published works, emerges from Walter's typewriter as if ventriloquized by another narrator, hidden and ironic; his moral tone of tragic strife gives way to Beckettian absurdity. Unfortunately, as Hendricks himself notes, Walter's interpolations are barely legible in the reproductions provided in *The Typist*. Benny Walter's texts should be read in the original, and until such time as his archive is made accessible to the public, the true import of the typist's work survives only in Hendricks' faithful annotations.

In Walter's late years he became almost completely reclusive. His neighbors remember a man humming to himself in his room and a silence broken more and more infrequently by the occasional tap of a key on his machine. Never fast as a typist – Walter pecked at the keyboard with his index fingers – he seems to have become almost paralyzed by the manuscript for the Bible. Shortly before Walter's death, Hendricks approached the typist on behalf of the Purgatory Press with a commission to prepare our book catalogue, but that typescript, regretfully, never saw the light of day. Among Walter's effects and unfinished projects from the period Hendricks uncovered a copyright application for an "O" with serifs; sketches on graph paper show a circle with a flat pedestal as if to stabilize it and crowned with a symmetrical line. Curiously, the siglum appears in none of Walter's texts, but toward the end the typist applied it to his own middle name. Musing on these clues, Hendricks ventures his speculations about Walter's frame of mind at the time of his death. The author suggests that we need not consider his end tragic or his work incomplete. Perhaps, Hendricks says, Walter saw his life's work finally realized in his idling Selectric, whose motionless typeball like his "O" with serifs came to represent to the typist the globe of the world become text.

329 pp.

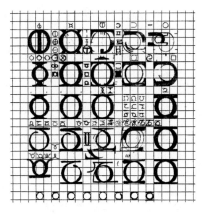

After the End

Red-eye

She has a wonderful app on her phone that lets her track in real time the progress of his flight. The plane is crossing the tip of Greenland now. Maybe out the window he can see Isua Nunaap? But he's probably asleep.

They spend a beautiful day together, no strife, no suspicion, no anxieties, no doubt. After so much time apart they had thought there might be trouble, but no. In the middle of the night he gets up quietly so as not to wake her, and when he comes back with a glass of water she is propped up in bed with the phone. She must be checking the progress of his flight.

Disclaimed

This story has been formatted for print and made to conform to a reader's attention span. No animals, genealogies, etc.

The language is English, the protagonist's only tongue, and in this respect the tale follows the conventions of most written works, which are typically monolingual, though in so doing it leaves out a host of other languages – Spanish during the journey to Spain, Italian in Italy – that swarm through the story, constituting, at times, the entire verbal subtext to Childress's thoughts and conversations.

As for the stray dogs sunning themselves at the Pompeii station, Anna's simple but pregnant statement, "I'm going to Capri," which Childress correctly reads as the declaration of a breakup with her boyfriend, but that he cannot fully parse for its intentions in his regard, would have signaled nothing worth noting, neither the cajoling inflection of an elderly person with leftover scraps to hand out nor the rising tone of a rambunctious child who might disturb their sleep.

Capri itself, the narrator concedes, is a standard *topos* of love and desire; readers tend to indulge stories that retread ordinary plot lines set there. But Childress's narrative of love and loss does not match romantic conventions; it is like a dream one recognizes to be a dream only by slipping it back into a manageable space, by concluding it all happened inside one's skull.

This raises a thorny problem, as dreams dilate in a space of time that can be very small indeed, sometimes mere milliseconds, opening up a different temporal dimension, as it were, like a purse with its edges in the here and now, but swelling in some other domain, while the object of the protagonist's fantasies is of course a person in her own right, with an existence of her own, which becomes increasingly apparent in the moments leading up to Childress's failure to act, when Anna finally passes the turnstile to set out on a life utterly separate from his.

Childress's almost inexplicable self-denial, the source of a tormenting regret that stays with him until his dying days (the period of the narrative's narration), comes back to him as he agonizes in a hospital bed: he sees the ferry trip to Capri as a metaphor of the deathward journey on which he is now embarked.

From his dying perspective, however, everything about that episode turns inside out. He realizes it was not love that he denied himself at the ferry terminal, but the promise of death, which Capri unknowingly came to represent to him following the trip to Pompeii. The vivacious Anna was an interference to this morbid desire, which he forestalled for a lifetime, all the while mourning a lost love he had deeply misrecognized, for like a person seen in a photographic negative, she (Anna) now represents to him a dealer of death.

The clue lies in a phrase spoken by an old woman clad in black mourning at the ferry terminal, telling the guard at the turnstile she was burying her husband that day: *Faccio seppellire mio marito oggi*, a phrase that Childress, knowing no Italian, could not have understood at the time, and, indeed, may not have heard at all, but which (improbably) persisted in his memory like an engraving to be deciphered only at death's door, along with everything else he did not know (the brushing by of the pickpocket, for example), and the world as a whole he had traversed like a tourist.

This suggests that the protagonist's story would best be rewritten in a tongue that his narrator, who does not presume omniscience, does not know, and which, like an insistent murmur accompanying Childress's musings and conversations, or, like meaningless subtitles constantly reabsorbing his story, only barely made themselves clear to him at the threshold of his final passage. To do so would be to use a language more alien even than Latin to the Pompeian dogs, an unheard-of language, because strictly inaudible, like the sounds of visitors that strike the petrified ears of bodies in the ruins, humans and dogs alike, buried by the kindly ash of Vesuvius (never mentioned in the text).

Killjoy

The joke never fails to amuse. That said, certain conditions have to be met. The audience should be neither abstracted, unconscious, preverbal, or mentally deficient. They should also be present for the telling, but if non-present, must be linked via some form of communication, e.g. television, telephone, radio, or internet. As a rule, the teller of the joke is alive, but if dead, still existing as a simulacrum, for instance as a recorded voice on tape, CD, or digital medium, or as a moving image in a film or video. The teller may also choose to convey the joke in print, in which case, as above, he or she may no longer be living when the joke is read, though to speak here of a "simulacrum" seems inappropriate, for reasons that are unclear but commonly accepted.

A child may sometimes tell the joke, but even if the delivery is adequate the effort is only humored, as they say. Similarly, a robot or other automated system might generate the appropriate word-chain without the desired effect. No computer program exists yet that can recognize a successful joke, and while a doll or toy clown sometimes has a voice-box that mimics the human laugh, like canned laughter on TV such responses are considered wholly artificial. Were the joke to appear from out of a random set of letters, a box of scrabble tiles, a hostage-taker's alphabet, a set of movable type, or in a sequence composed by the proverbial typing monkeys, the result would likely be less funny than disturbing.

One virtue of the joke is its brevity; it can be told in one breath. However, being made up of several phrases, it could be conceivably delivered in separate parts, for example, with a pause in the middle, during which the teller might take a bite of a cracker, or sip his drink, only so long as to whet the listener's interest, or break off momentarily to pick up his cell phone, perhaps to mute the ringer, but if expecting important news might suspend the telling a while longer, most likely to the detriment of the joke. Delay, however, could be exploited as a purpose in and of itself. A person of infinite means might choose to deliver one word of the joke each time he circled the Earth; arriving by plane after each trip, he would convoke his listeners to hear the next word, or even, in order to extend the journey – but why? – the next letter or syllable, though no doubt the listeners would grow impatient, or would have heard the joke elsewhere by that time, since it is so popular, and popular jokes travel quickly, faster even than planes, in fact.

Everyone recalls the time and place they first heard the joke, and some may also remember what they were doing when, while perhaps rehearsing it in their mind, they felt a layer of meaning peel away to reveal some hidden truth, like a body lying in the weeds. So for each person it has a special meaning, utterly private, though everyone shares in a common recollection, as with the day of the (first) Kennedy assassination. No doubt Freud's insight remains as true today as it did a hundred years ago: a joke is passed from person to person like news from the battlefront.

Of course the joke is funniest if never heard before. Like many jokes, though, it bears repeating, but not right away, unless the listener or listeners failed to hear it, due to some noise, momentary inattention, or other interruption, e.g. the cat knocking over a vase, ice-cream truck, or even, since the TV is always on, a joke on a sitcom, in which case the joke is interrupted by a joke, never auspicious. The passage of time may work to the benefit of the joke, which thereby reclaims some of its novelty, and a change of context can also warrant a retelling. One cannot, however, call one's friends into an adjoining room to hear the joke again. On the other hand, one might tell the same joke to the identical group of friends some years later in the very same room. In this case, the retelling might carry a dividend of nostalgia, while the joke itself may have paled imperceptibly in humor, but not so much as to make it pleasureless. The forgetful and amnesiac would enjoy it perhaps most. Beyond a certain point, such as one's own life-span, the joke will likely have no further value, and cultures of the future, whether living the horrors we expect or an unforeseen earthly paradise, probably would have no use for the joke, assuming it were comprehensible to them and passed down in a language they understood.

Do angels tell jokes? One hardly imagines them snickering, sniggering, snorting, or guffawing, all of which imply some malice or sarcasm. And though they might be considered to giggle or chuckle, what humor would they find in the topic of the joke (death)? Placid, indolent, mostly silent, they are no doubt more like animals, or rather household pets, the ones who are glad to see us happy, but alarmed to hear us laugh.

Unanswered

People always ask me where I'm going. Where are you going, Mike, they ask, Where are you off to, Ed, or Sandra, or Doña Elena Torres (names have been changed to protect the innocent). Which raises a question of its own: why names when you can use a number, in the manner, for instance, of the Popes? Innocent I, Innocent II, Innocent III (author of *On the Misery of the Human Condition*), Innocents IV, V, VI, VII, VIII (launched trials against witches), Innocents IX, X, XI, XII, XIII, Innocent XIV (antipope).

Where are you going? Where are you going? And less often, but still too much for my liking, Where are you going with all this? I know a rhetorical question, it's like a hand that yanks away when your fingers meet. But have I ever been so bold as to extend a mitt, or even lift a finger, tempting as that is, if you recall the portrait of John the Baptist? As for pointing something out, never tempted, though it often seems my index is holding a place after everyone's shut the book.

It's not as if I were sitting at the bus stop, waiting for a bus that never comes. Those stiff benches and their grudging hospitality. Or at the airport, why would I be at the airport, even if, true enough, my bags are always at my side. And do you think they'd let me in? With my shaved scalp (head lice? mange?) or long, matted hair, deplorable in a woman, only somewhat less so in a man? Let's say, for argument's sake, I made it out to the gate, where fabulous windows look out on the most desolate and inspiring views. Would they pity me then, peering out of their portholes as they taxi away? Or as they nose into the terminal, wondering, if they've never arrived here before, Is this what they all look like, the people of X? Is this person typical, a template of the population at large, a racial exemplum? Do they all jot things on a smudged stenographer's notepad? They'd like to rap on the window, I bet, like kids at the zoo, frustrated at my grand and alien self-possession.

Patience is my only tutor. Never looking up, even when people yell from their cars. Is it my fault that my arm, once it lets go my bags, tends to stick out from my body, and my fist (cramped, not clenched) with my opposable digit points into the air?

*

Why are they so happy? you ask yourself. Or rather, you don't, but it nags at you, or visits your thoughts at night, your head in the mattress, if you can call that thinking.

They come up from the valley, walking single file if it suits them, but more often in a disordered band, and emerge from the trees, scattering onto the open fields, then later as the season advances onto the higher alps, among the lupens, the gentians and the edelweiss, crushing them in their teeth, shitting every which where. The sun rains down on them from the snowfields. But they duck their heads, snorting, and when they lie on the grass, sated but chewing still, their eyes betray no sense of irony.

Rumination, it's called. True enough, they chew their cud, and like us they heave up things that are better spit out, but they keep turning it over in their teeth, grinding it down in stubborn mouths that never utter a word. You might think they'd produce only bile as dark as ink, but, unaccountably, their milk is almost impeccably white. Sometimes one of them might have the delicacy of preserving the unique savor of a mountain blossom, the special *terroir* of her private alp, but all is poured into giant vats, diluted into a common stock, maybe thereby approaching the abstract anonymity of each animal's constant self-negation.

They say their farts will melt the glaciers. So they will no doubt climb higher, onto those sublime fields of rock and gravel, fertilizing them, spawning new and loftier fields, all the while ruminating, so they say. We will be baking in hell. And maybe then they'll go higher still, growing long legs and nimble hooves, dancing on the peaks now, bells tinkling, where we hear them but can't reach. And then what will we drink?

*

What's that noise, she suddenly asks in the middle of dinner. The clinking stops and everyone turns to her, then toward the big picture window where the five of us are reflected in the glare. A hum of traffic heading to the foothills. The fan turning as usual. Tinnitus, but that's in my head. Then she laughs and the banter picks up again. I should mention that I had loved her once, and she let me down gracefully, as if I'd never made a move. Her husband is charming, a good friend, and the evening is convivial, a perfect success. Okay, why exaggerate, the wine did its thing.

Should the bachelor leave first or last? A conundrum. When I finally get to the car I realize I've forgotten my hat. So I go back up to the house and find myself in front of that big picture window. She and her husband are clearing the table in silence under the blazing chandelier. I stand there for a moment in the dark, uncertain, then turn back without knocking, wishing I hadn't seen anything. And of course I hadn't, what was there to see?

*

When did you get hurt? I'm imagining a doctor who gave a damn. As for where, the question's impertinent, I'm patently wrecked. At least I'm spared the indignity of caring, no, I take it back, of believing in cures, or rather, of making others believe, which is different, I think, and worse, I'm sure.

Crybaby wants his milk? Uh-uh. I'm going back even further, but try as I might I can get only so far. A wizened face appears for its first interview. The parents say he's crying over his happy security, his warm nest, his lost solipsistic paradise, poor thing.

And so, yoked into language, our cries make sense. No one gives meaning to a log that falls down and goes thump.

*

Who took the keys? he yells at his wife. No answer. They're right in front of her, on the table by the alcove. But she just stands there, considering their house planted on a drifting continent, on a spinning globe, in a dizzying orbit around a star that is speeding away.

*

A question on the tip of my tongue, if that is my tongue, if it's me, if it's even a question, dry, unpalatable, thinner than the proverbial wafer.

Riders

I was twelve when my father asked me what I wanted to be when I grew up. He was bent over the kitchen sink fiddling with something.

"A writer," I said cautiously.

"A rider…" he echoed and grunted in approval without turning around.

He must have pictured it in his head: striking out onto the open road, never mind family and home, becoming one with a forward impulse, becoming sheer movement. He must have thought I admired the neighbor's motorbike when he came back from weekend trips, sometimes with a pack of buddies, chrome flashing, engines idling in the driveway. Late at night they rumbled off and rattled things in the cupboards. Would that have woken him up, did he fret about his middle age? I suppose the neighbor's bike was in front of him right then, out the window above the sink. And so he could easily imagine it: a boy in his room looking out the window at those studded-leather emissaries of freedom.

I didn't notice the changes right away. Or rather, the changes were caught up in a crowd of others that shouldered them aside. Adam's apple, paper route, weekly allowance. I hardly had time for reading anymore. How did I get the new nickname? Since when did he give me that pat on the head, and how long had it been since I flinched? I saw us for the first time as a pair, for some reason as cut-out silhouettes: him, enormous in his eternal baggy shorts and team jersey; me, thin, tiny, nervous, like one of those creatures just emerged from a burrow and scenting the air for danger.

Next birthday a motorcycle materialized in the garage: a vintage Honda Sport 90, not much faster than a scooter but styled like a toy version of the hulking 750 he had bought himself. Along with a helmet from my anxious mother, it was my only gift that year. The stunned look on my face was taken as a sign of unutterable joy. Prodded on by my father, who had to kick-start the bike for me, I practiced riding short jolting stretches up and down the driveway, all that my mother would allow just yet. The bike being lightweight, it didn't break any bones by falling on me, which was every time I stopped or turned, but I couldn't easily crawl out from under it either. When it went quiet outside, my parents must have thought I was studying the manual, but I was more likely pinned under the machine, eying the clouds or the clods, depending, and after that welcome respite finally crying out like a cat stuck in a tree.

I had been subscribed to motorsport magazines that I was expected to read cover to cover, and my father called me down whenever a race came on TV, all with a firm but benevolent attitude. I was a good listener, because never understanding the words coming out of his mouth, or their purpose, I was on constant alert, all ears, all eyes. In the past, my father had resented the daily chore of shaping me into something like a boy, but now he took my laziness for a lack of confidence that needed gentle support. He showed none of his former impatience with my lack of coordination, my clumsiness, my overall fleshly weakness, and seemed to have an unshakable faith in my potential. It was as if he had had a conversion, was reversing course in rearing me, and had decided, without the least regret or disappointment, that I was, after all, a girl, someone to be treated with extra care, whose failings in manly tasks were endearing, and whose highest purpose was to embody all the contradictory meanings of filial love. It was hard to resist. I accepted the bond that formed between us, weighing its benefits against the warping it would do to my nature, a calculation familiar to man's best friend. It was our honeymoon of sorts. If only it weren't for the motorcycles, I thought.

One day, perplexed as always at these phenomena, I finally traced them back to their cause. My eye had landed on the cover of a garish *Rider* magazine, one that was hiding a *New Yorker* inside and, reading the title as if for the first time I flashed back to the scene that had apparently sealed my fate. The misunderstanding was so simple it could be easily cleared up but, waiting for the best chance to confront my father, I put it off day after day, slinking in his shadow. Meanwhile, he seemed absorbed by endless new tasks and I couldn't catch his eye. When I finally did, I was held back by a firm stare. He already knew. Why, then, the continued pretense? But how to take back all those gestures of trust and affection? A prison door seemed to be closing on us; I told myself this would be the time to break the silence, to set things straight, but the decisive moment passed and things went on as before, like a stalemate, or like a marriage in which the roles are so set that a mask can fall off to zero effect.

I had always been insomniac but now with my fresh crop of anxieties I slept less than ever. This meant that in spite of my new obligations I had more time than ever for study, which was cause to rejoice, though during the day I was also more feeble and tired, if that were possible. Due to my constant spills I developed a morbid fear of crushing my head and took to wearing my helmet at all times, visor flipped up while I pored over my Whitman, Thoreau, or Dickinson. The helmet had the added benefit of muffling the outside world, and I made great strides in my sense of prosody as my father clattered in the toolbox, assembling and dismantling our bikes. Sometimes their parts lay spread out for complex repairs, and I was glad it would be weeks before we rode again. The arrival of snow was an even greater blessing; I tapped out meters with gloved fingers: *Le vierge, le vivace et le bel aujourd'hui.* I owe to my father's canvas drop cloth, with its bolts and disassembled parts, my insights into Mallarmé, Rimbaud, and Surrealist *automatismes*, texts more approachable when I pictured them, daydreaming, as symbols scattered on the garage floor. I became the most patient of apprentices, sitting cross-legged, uncomplaining, my nose buried in some tome I couldn't read slowly enough, and which seemed to exist, like all of my books and things and even my own puny self, in a determinedly blind spot of my father's visual world. But how could I know, not being a father, whether this was because he was bound to some higher paternal order of duty, or because the oracular power of his fateful word had in fact trumped mine, so that I truly existed only as his vision of my future self, which was taking shape regardless of my will?

During this period I finally found my balance and rode the cycle with a measure of confidence, always imagining it completely smashed to pieces, but how to survive that sudden deconstruction kept me baffled a long time. I rode as if frozen at that impossible moment when all would stop for me, but at other times pictured the parts of the engine in slow motion, like symbols caught in the swirling geometries of cubist art. I followed my father on short outings, then longer rides into the fields, and when my license finally came I was enlisted in the mystifying duty of covering every road possible, near and far, maybe to confirm their existence, or perhaps because he had reason to doubt the maps? And why the empty banter with other riders we met, which must have hidden a secret code? They answered my gaping silence with friendly winks. We're going up to Chilliwack, my father would announce, referring to our next projected trip, and when I mouthed those very words to myself en route, they served just as well in the present. This temporal distortion gave me fresh insight into the force of my father's will, so strong it could bend time itself into a seamless flowing now.

Days stretched into months and years. My bike was eventually traded up to a 125, then a respectable 250, and as a matter of course our trips extended to cross-state overnights, the requisite pilgrimage to the Black Hills, and the inevitable continental traverse, when I finally enrolled in a college on the other coast where my cycle was doomed to rust in the alley by the dormitory's kitchen door.

My homebody friends are always amazed to learn that I have biked up into the Yukon, that I have followed the Rockies from the Arctic to Sonora, that I have traveled through places in the Deep South that seemed lost in some other era. But all those places passed by my consciousness like things seen through a screen (which they were) and heard through a thick protective layer (true as well), while I myself lay coiled up in back of my eyes, a half-sleeping fetus. Tailing behind, more passenger than rider, I had learned to write in my head and store it there safely for later. Another gift I got from my father, or maybe just from the comforting sight of his enormous back and hunched shoulders blocking the destination from view.

Cameo

She used to tell a story about how she met Alfred Hitchcock when she was a girl. It was at Glendale station, a Mission-style building on a dusty, sun-blasted stretch of track just north of Los Angeles. Her mother noticed a portly bald man sitting on a bench in the shade, and when he stood up to greet someone she followed him with her eyes and said to her husband, "Isn't that Alfred Hitchcock?" She'd turned away in speaking so she had to repeat the question, more loudly this time, but she was still staring in the famous man's direction and he must have overheard it. Then it was time to board the train and her parents began collecting their bags. Suddenly the girl remembered the stuffed bunny she had left on a bench inside the station. She ran back into the building and nearly banged into the old man on her way out. She looked up. "That would be *Sir* Alfred," he said to the girl, deadpan, bending over slightly and mouthing his words in a slow, deliberate manner that made everything around her come to a stop. There were wooden beams spanning the ceiling, patterned with colored motifs.

She wondered afterwards whether the story stayed with her because it was the last trip she took together with her mother and father. In fact things had already been unraveling at her aunt's in San Diego. By the time they got to San Francisco her parents were just going through the motions. "She'd like to see Coit Tower," her mother said, without asking the girl. "She hasn't seen the Golden Gate." The bridge was red and neither her father or mother could say why. Back in Portland it was separation then divorce.

Years later she followed a boyfriend down to the Bay Area. It was 1987. He dealt coke and speed and took her to parties all over, from Sausalito to San José, and from the Oakland Hills to Pacific Heights. She was a pretty enough girl, but young and awkward; she watched the other girls and tried to do like them, but this only made her more self-conscious. At such times she would remember her story about Sir Alfred. It let her inflate her California history, her family connections. She dropped place names but left out the dates.

One night a boy from Mill Valley latched onto the story and wouldn't let go. He was a college student and film buff with oversize black glasses and a fierce coke habit that made him talk a mile a minute. "You know," he said, "when Hitchcock was knighted by the Queen he only had a few months to live." She hadn't considered that. "It was a pretty narrow window of time," he insisted. "From New Year's to April, 1980." She had told him the scene in Glendale took place around Easter, which was how she recalled it, but the way he went at her with questions she couldn't be sure. It might have been earlier, or possibly later, if that even made sense. Then he pointed out something she already knew, or that someone had told her before: the director always appeared in his own movies, sneakily, in the background. And in one case – this was a scene in a station too – he could be spotted rolling along in a wheelchair, then suddenly jumping up to shake someone's hand, a miraculous recovery or some kind of practical joke. You missed it usually, focused on the plot, he said, and laughed, squinting behind his glasses. But then why the distraction, she wondered helplessly, wishing now she had never brought the story up. As he went on about films she hadn't seen and names she didn't know she wore a smile that felt like it was pasted there. She avoided him the rest of the night.

Her boyfriend had known her former boyfriend; one day he pulled his car over and gave her a lift and that was that. Her mother was dead set against the boy, but she felt an amazing lightness and freedom, realizing everything that was habit and routine and obligation could change in a flash. More important, she took it as proof she could be discovered, but she was super-stitious on this point. It would only be possible, she told herself, when she wasn't paying attention, when she was just being herself, looking the other way, and this meant she always had to put the wish out of her head, though not so much that she could ever forget it. Her luck might have been better in Los Angeles. As it happened, her boyfriend's work kept him in the Bay Area before sending them north again on the freeway.

Drugs took their toll. In Seattle it was heroin. In Vancouver her boyfriend did well at first then learned some hard lessons about turf. The lack of money turned him mean; he warned her she would have to work the streets. One morning she opened her eyes and saw a skein of fog snaking past the window. It brushed the tops of the tall red container cranes standing sentry at the docks. For a moment she believed she was back in San Francisco.

There's no view of the sea from the Downtown Eastside. Across the city a break of blue sky hung low over the Strait of Georgia. Out on English Bay a giant ship lay at anchor, motionless, like the famous final sequence in Hitchcock's *Marnie*.

Y2K

I wonder when I first heard the name Jean Pellegrino. Does it matter? By that time her work had taken on a life of its own: anonymous, ubiquitous, iconic, due to her creative flair, and also, maybe more importantly, force of circumstance. But I'll forgo the disquisition on higher laws.

At the '99 Venice Biennale, her first major show, Pellegrino exhibited two sculptures in the American Pavilion, each inspired by features of the urban landscape. One piece was modeled on a so-called Jersey wall, the concrete blocks used for dividing traffic lanes or bordering work sites and empty lots. Pellegrino's version of this homely thing was cast in ice and lit from within like an oversize angular light bulb. In a technical and stylistic feat the artist molded her piece in a layer of ice as thin as wax paper. The fragile sculpture was housed in a sound-proofed refrigerated gallery and could be approached by only a half-dozen viewers at a time, wearing slippers and confined to felted walkways.

In the next room she displayed the work that made her name: a humble metal pedestrian barrier fence of a kind familiar to political protesters and gawkers at street parades. The sculpture was wrapped in gold leaf and lit from above like a precious jewel. Rather than duplicate an actual fence Pellegrino cast an original of her own, lending it a gangly form and pocked surface some critics compared to Giacometti. As with her subsequent showings, Pellegrino called the Venice installation "provisional," since her plans for the piece were more ambitious, not to say presumptuous. Mock-ups of her intended display setting are based on Napoleon's tomb at the Church of the Invalides in Paris, where visitors on a marble gallery circle around the emperor's sarcophagus, which, while well below them in the rotunda's center, continues somehow to dominate the entire space. The exhibition catalogue cites from Pellegrino's fruitless correspon-dence with the French Defense Ministry, where she pleads that they remove the Emperor's remains for the purpose of displaying her work.

Never having gone to the Biennale, I refer to the record. But looking at the catalogue brings back memories of my own: summer 1968, when, too young to catch the echoes of the spring revolts, I stayed with my family in a pension near the vast, vacant esplanade of the Invalides; 1983, when I lost a semester at the Sorbonne closed by student strikes; 1986, a year of aimless art studies; 1993, when I enrolled in a philosophy program, soon abandoned for politics; 1997, now a tourist, standing with a guidebook at Napoleon's tomb. Pellegrino's biography shows she was in Paris some of that time. We must have crossed paths, though the idea only comes to me as I browse the catalogue, picturing myself with the guidebook in hand, leaning on the balustrade, my back to the author of the Code, the one who said, "I am the Revolution," and wound up in a church. The text said the emperor lies in six coffins, each tucked inside another like Russian dolls, and all enclosed in the huge red sarcophagus. I remember wondering or dreaming about those coffins stretching out in a lengthening series, growing larger or maybe increasingly small, the kind of passing thought you tend to brush away, but probably so as not to doubt reality.

Everyone knows the fortunes of Pellegrino's Venice sculptures are linked to the publicity they gained when, one week after the closing of the Biennale, the World Trade Organization protests erupted in Seattle. Golden barrier fences spontaneously appeared all over the city, and in the following years protesters with spray paint made them regular fixtures at WTO events and leftist demonstrations worldwide. A runner-up for the Pulitzer Prize in photography in 2000 showed a pair of riot cops behind a golden fence, one looking down at his shiny palms, the other pointing a gilt finger at the camera. Paul Weightman's *How Soon is Today*, the bible of anarchists and the anti-systemic intelligentsia, famously sported the image of a golden fence on its cover. Pellegrino launched the first of her copyright cases over this use of her image and lost, but coverage of the story only raised her profile.

In 2001, apotheosis. The artist displayed a big sculpture in the central atrium of the Guggenheim in New York: a three-storey gold ladder, tapering slightly toward the top and missing all but the upper five rungs. Like her barrier fence the ladder was hand-forged, and one almost imagined the earlier sculpture having been stretched like taffy to the length of a fire ladder or telescoping like the spidery legs of Dalì's impossible elephants. Ironically, given her recent copyright case, Pellegrino's useless ladder was adopted by an investment firm as the image for an ad campaign on retirement portfolios. Even more surprising was the slogan that accompanied the ads, which inadvertently, or so it seemed, echoed the title of Weightman's book: "How soon is retirement?" This time, taking the firm to court, Pellegrino won and garnered a large settlement, said to be in the millions. A second case followed within the investment firm, which accused its art director of knowingly and maliciously provoking the lawsuit due to "subversive intent of an anarchist nature." The case failed though, and when the art director later flaunted his political stripes, he claimed that he became radicalized out of disillusionment with the corporate world because of the abuse he had suffered at trial.

At some point during the opening of her Guggenheim show, Pellegrino wandered off from the patrons, connoisseurs and hangers-on, and in a corner of the atrium began flinging a heavy rope into the air as if trying and failing to catch it on an invisible target above her, a performance that became known as "Sky Hook." I would have liked to have seen her there. But who would I have been in that crowd? In my mind I see her as a child with a jump rope glumly tracing a circle around her body, or floating in an orb like a figure from Hieronymus Bosch. After a year in which she mysteriously left the public spotlight, Pellegrino moved "Sky Hook" to her private gallery in Chelsea where she has devoted herself exclusively to her performance, which she insists on keeping up, she says, "until it works."

Several museums and collectors vied for the purchase of Pellegrino's gold ladder, but she chose to loan it to the city of Paris, where she had it installed on a busy thoroughfare, leaning against a high, sooty, nearly black stone wall still bearing the remnants of a guard tower in a part of the city's ancient fortifications. Located on the Rue du Louvre right across from the Commodity Exchange, the ladder seemed to launch a hopeless assault on a fading emblem of royal power. The piece was affixed by only four simple clamps and insured for the value of its gold leaf alone. Occasionally a policeman would have to shoo away youths who tried to scrape a flake off the surface. I remember being stood up there by a date. At the time the ladder seemed like a disused Christmas decoration or something left behind by a parade float. After a few years, Hans Köhler, a German art historian, noted a slight bowing in the long legs of the ladder. What he speculated on the spot soon turned out to be true: the pliable metal ladder was made of solid gold, and weighing as it did nearly half a ton, could be conservatively valued at some twenty million dollars.

Köhler's discoveries provoked a sensation in the art world. The scholar contacted Pellegrino for an interview, but rebuffed by the vow of silence that accompanied her "Sky Hook" performance, he followed leads about the sale of a large amount of bullion to an anonymous buyer in New York. The gold came from various sellers but all derived from the Spanish Federal Reserve and dated from the conquest of South America. Pellegrino had apparently insisted on using gold usurped from the Aztec and Inca Empires; the ingots she melted down for her sculpture were once sacred relics of civilizations destroyed for God and profit. This lofty symbolism soon gave way to tabloid scandal, though, as Pellegrino's family clan in Paramus sued for control of her assets on the grounds of the artist's alleged mental incompetence, blocking her plans to donate the ladder to the Gold Museum in Bogotà.

Pellegrino's gallery is a brick cube of a building, once a cardboard warehouse next to the gritty High Line in Chelsea. With the opening of the pedestrian greenway on the former train trestle people can now lean over the railing and peer down at her workspace, or rather its blank exterior wall. This side of the Millennium, gentrification has passed a squeegee over the whole area. Behind the gallery, though, your typical alley: dumpsters, greasy doorsteps, grated windows. Like the alley off First Avenue in Seattle where I ducked in when the protest line broke. They – I mean we – should have put up more resistance. When people started scattering I took a right turn into the alley. Someone was slinking behind a dumpster, anonymous, long shaggy hair and beard. We huddled together in a doorway as if stuck in a broken elevator. Nothing like the '60s, he kept saying. When things died down he opened his pack and said he needed to lighten his load. Help yourself to anything, he said. For the sake of camaraderie I looked at his grubby hoard. There was a spray can in a paper bag. Metallic gold. I meant to use it to tag my ex's house, he said, but I'm no stalker. Besides, I've got a restraining order. Another reason not to get too close to the cops, he added, but now he seemed to be talking to himself.

At the far end of the alley you could hear the muffled sound of street fighting. Anachronism of clattering hooves. I thought of a scene from *Sentimental Education* where Frédéric catches sight of a battle on a barricade while he's minding his own petty business. A twinge of regret I was letting the revolution pass me by. Doesn't it always? 1830. 1848. 1871. 1917. 1968. 1999. Six coffins, one inside the other. But still no sarcophagus.

The Seattle protests would fizzle like the Y2K bug, though no one banking on catastrophe could be let down by the coming decade. Meanwhile, under the High Line, time stands still. No interviews. No pictures. No video. The most recent photo of the artist shows her looking prematurely aged, but with the grim determination of an anchorite.

It was the end of the first day of the protests. Maybe that night a traffic camera was tilted down on me when I found a metal barrier fence splayed on the pavement, waiting for the assumption.

Echos [sic]

My dearest, in your absence I take rambles along the shore, and sometimes up to Vandoeuvres and beyond, pausing in spots that evoke the wilds of the northern heath. The summer has been so frightfully damp and dreary that the dear land of the thistle is called up quite unbidden by memory and fancy. But the vines look forlorn and I fear the wine will be poor this year. When may we expect your return?

Sent from my BlackBerry

Today I fancied hearing your voice, dearest, pealing on the crags above Argentière. But in truth, my Echo, I should make a poor Narcissus here. No water but which leaps, plashes and cascades down, even among the high alpine pastures. Where a pool sometimes lingers in a vale it takes the color of verdigris on Grecian bronze, and I am reminded that Virgil's glad realm lies just beyond a gleaming ridge. Why, then, did the ancients neglect these lofty haunts?

Sent from my iPhone

No, not Echo, dearest, but perhaps a banshee! Today I was at the foot of the Salève, whose great scarred cliff rears up from the valley like an enormous Hadrian's wall. I had chased a vision from Plainpalais, stumbling like a ragged madwoman across fields and woods. I considered the silty waters of the Arve rushing down from Chamonix, and beneath the mountain I saw with double sight a vision of my monster clambering up its banded granite face, while by my side a tragic Prometheus cradled a young innocent. Do I have the strength to put this to paper? Must I bring down that wall or risk myself in an escalade?

Sent from my BlackBerry

On the *Mer de Glace*! Unsung marvels of this frozen cataract's crags, crevasses and tilted seracs. In the maw of a dim blue chapel the walls pulse with the groans and sighs of souls in limbo. How long this motionless journey?

Sent from my iPhone

My dearest, still dreary here, but admirably green! Loneliness and nostalgia – not for home but a more familiar exile. Scotland, so dear to my heart, I knew in two guises, each defined by your absence: the first, when it was haunted by what, in my innocence, I never knew I lacked; the second, after our meeting, when that lack had a name and a face, giving meaning, but not presence, to the lonely moors, the standing stones, the keening wind. We loved one another in the interval.

Sent from my BlackBerry

First night above the trees, far beyond the trappings of mere life. Rapture of the early dawn in a landscape that evokes the furthest septentrion, yet fanned by a kindly Aeolus. Have never felt the South so near as in this Arctic waste, and am sorely tempted to follow the meridian.

Sent from my iPhone

Dearest, John says that beneath Lake Geneva is a chasm like the hull of an enormous sunken ship. I believe I shall never view its calm surface quite the same again. It seems our gentle lake was carved by glaciers that have since withdrawn to the mountains. But why did they go and will they ever return?

Sent from my BlackBerry

plunging headwaters o'er

Sent from my iPhone

Dreadful dream last night. I found myself among the vineyards by the house; the grapes were full and ready for the harvest. It was a fine late summer day, though the stillness all about seemed like the hush that follows a battle's awful clamor. Upon waking I could not dispel the sense of ravages hidden under the simple appearance of things, and now, I know not why, that ghastly hush seems instead to portend ravages to come.

Sent from my BlackBerry

Have grown reclusive. Pass the days at my desk with the lake as sole companion, and come nightfall, my flickering image takes the place of the view in the panes.

Sent from my BlackBerry

Troubled by your silence of late. Preoccupied with the thought that the Scotland I feel here in Cologny is that of my first visit – the one unknown to you, as you were unknown to me.

Sent from my BlackBerry

Laboring still on this lifeless thing in which I scarcely know myself. I doubt not you shall make the mountains sing, while I must content myself with stubborn prose, mud and mire that I would were clay.

Sent from my BlackBerry

Dear friend, I write at Mary's urging to inquire of your status ("Have you influence, Polidori?"). Upon your return you should find things much as you left them, if a trifle more gloomy. The weather has been singularly grey, and the needle on the barometer, which I consult at all times, lies as still as the hand on a broken clock. I am inclined to believe that the creators of the thing, through some odd perversity, meant only to show us what we already know, and to provoke the needless gesture of tapping on the glass.

Sent from my Android device

Voice over

Michael Winter is not having sex. He's been dating a girl all freshman year, but their physical contact stops short of coitus. It can be concluded that Michael is a virgin, an anomaly to his friends and peers though not aberrant in the larger scheme of things. This illuminates a general law of phenomena, namely that what is remarkable is only so in its given context – in this case, a California university campus, its student body and environs, but also the suburb of a small town in upstate New York just a stone's throw from the River Hudson.

At the start of fall semester Michael made his way past Telegraph's retro wares and hippie arcana, holdovers from Berkeley's radical days. He was too busy to concern himself with the protests and bullhorn-toting evangelists on campus. The freshman's first months of college were a headlong rush of discoveries and a corresponding repudiation of his background, an affective state that may be captured in an image: Michael winging home for Christmas and gazing out from the plane, meanwhile humming a song that evoked the same view and scorned the lives of people down below. The tune was by Talking Heads, a quirky art-rock band Michael had learnt of in high school, at one of the very places reviled by the song, an irony lost on him, however, and seemingly requiring another level of perspective, as if from someone orbiting above.

Ladies and Gentlemen, the airport nearest Michael's hometown is Albany International, and a plane's approach or departure can involve wide arcs and banking turns that take the craft east across the river. Even when the flight is to or from points west, a plane may circle high over Saratoga Springs to the north, from where one can spot the lower tip of Lake George, whose name at times struck Michael as faintly odd, as though the Hudson might be called the Henry, or Lake George his own given name. This is where Michael went to sailing camp one hot summer when he was ten years old. If he were to make the effort, he could no doubt bring back to memory the name of a campmate, the notorious Alan Springer, connected to an incident there that Michael sometimes replayed in his mind.

One afternoon early in the camp session Michael came to a halt in front of the women's restroom. Public lavatories have labels of all kinds, but the door he was facing read "M" like the one adjacent. The reason soon became clear: some prankster had inverted the "W" by unscrewing the letter, reversing it, and mounting it that way on the door. A gash on the letter betrayed the act.

Planted barefoot in front of the restrooms Michael reflected on several things in the space of what must have been less than a minute. First of all, the inverted "W," while apparently the same as its neighboring "M," was in fact quite different, having sharp crests and diagonals unlike the latter's serifs and vertical columns. And since the "W" now covered a different surface area, closer inspection confirmed the grimy trace of its former outline on the door. Michael then pictured the inverted letter returning to its original position, but in so doing he saw not only the letter but the entire building (a freestanding cabin with shiplap siding) turn on its end, then fully upside down. Gravity likewise reversing its directional force, though without affecting Michael himself, all things came unstuck, flew into the air, the picnic tables, the hated sail bags, his fellow camp mates, while inside the bathrooms, no doubt, seats snapped open and toilet paper rolls unspooled skyward. Only then, while glued to the ground, as bikes, skateboards, flipflops, oars and canoes scattered into the air, never to return, perhaps doomed to circle the Earth forever as space junk, was Michael able to read in their proper order the initials of his own name on the cabin's twin doors.

None of which would have proved so memorable had he not turned at that point to see Gabriel, a camp counselor, standing amid the cataracting debris, his two eyes holding him like a deer in their sights, a small boy with his finger on the door to the ladies' room. The counselor called out Michael's name with the rising tone that marks a query, the property also of sonorous bodies in accelerating approach. On his face was a look of complicity turning to consternation, but without blame, then pity or disappointment, though Michael couldn't fathom why, as the older man came to recognize behind the frozen tableau the simple nature of the prank the boy was trying to decode. And now, after a delay, as if transported outside himself and into the past, the very recent past, but one that would keep trailing behind him at all times, the boy realized he should have been trying to figure something out, something else, and may in fact have been doing so, but was distracted from that purpose. The look on the counselor's face seemed a confirmation of his failure, but rather than provide him means for self-reflection, those eyes were like the alarm that dispels the dream. From then on the counselor showed him special affection, often only with a particularly attentive gaze Michael studiously ignored.

Gabriel seemed a different person when some days later he stood up stiffly to make an announcement at dinner, scolding Alan Springer in front of the entire bowed assembly after the boy had been exposed by a confidant.

As for the rest of the month at camp, Ladies and Gentlemen, long hours becalmed, marshmallows, sticky nights, all is without notable episodes, without drama, without incident.

Recycler

Whole weeks go by when all I manage to do is set the trash can out in the street. Tuesday is pickup day, and as I cart the can out I tell myself, Remember to cart the trash can out, meaning next week. And a few times during the week after I drop something in the can I remind myself again, Tuesday is garbage day, cart the can out Tuesday morning, or to be on the safe side, Monday night. Although on two or three occasions, giving in to doubt, temptation, or something preternatural, I have even carted it out on Sunday, hoping not to run into anyone going to church, or coming back, either way it could jar with their finery: white gloves, pretty hats, good shoes, smart jackets. In which case do I sleep better on Sunday and Monday nights? I always sleep well, no problem there.

Once upon a time, I'd think of my loved ones and ask, Where are they now? Then the answer came, Oh. But as for my stuff, who can say? The razor that left a scar under my ear? The pencil that wrote, Don't expect me back? The eraser that rubbed it out? Word is we'll get recycling service one day, so I'll have another can to fill. The news left me bewildered and somehow offended, like a young girl who's been propositioned or a diner who, leaving through the back, passes a rank and steaming trash bin.

I could use a datebook to keep track of my Tuesdays. Or I might put a post-it note where I couldn't miss it, but then wouldn't I have to remember to put up the post-it note? Of course it could be there all the time, say right on the bathroom mirror, but I'm not geriatric, even though what stares back at me is no treat for the eyes. So instead Tuesday remains on my mind, beginning Tuesday itself, which in my imaginary calendar is the start of the week, and unlike your calendars, which have rows of weeks one after the other, mine resembles a clock face, with Tuesday at the top, like high noon.

The middle of the week is a fall from grace, sweeping down

toward the Sabbath until Tuesday exerts its attraction again, yanking the week back upward like the pull of the moon. Once at the top, the calendar comes almost to a complete halt, and poised like a pendulum seems for lack of moment about to fall backward, then finally creeps past that inverted nadir, impossibly slowly, like Tuesday itself, which tends to drag on forever, especially when the garbage men are late, something that happens annoyingly often.

Why take back something you've done, or spoken, or thought, it's out there. I'll admit it then, I've even set the can by the curb on Saturday. Obviously that's pushing it, and illegal besides. But when I dragged the can out to the street on that designated day of rest, I had the feeling I was about to cross the Rubicon. After all, what if I spanned the whole weekend, going back into Friday, and then, no doubt, drawn on irresistibly, even further still? Checking the impulse, but actually savoring the transgression I was fulfilling in my mind, I measured the scope of my ambition. For if I crossed the Rubicon, or is it the Acheron, wouldn't I be moving backward in time and into the previous week? How could I not go as far as Tuesday, overlapping last week's trash day? I will have taken today's garbage and disposed of it in the past.

I had discovered another week, unknown to your calendars, stretching out like an unexplored continent. I was tempted to give new names to the days I'd discovered, adopting the language of maids and conquistadors: *Viernes*, for Friday, no doubt because of the virginal quality of the day I was set to claim; *Jueves*, for the egg-like perfection of its untampered secrets; *Miercoles*, bristling with fearsome mystery as I neared my destination; and finally, *Martes*, blunt, simple, and self-effacing, like death itself, whose name it suggests on the sly, as if words suddenly stuttered and failed in the face of my supreme achievement. When I drag the can out to the street that Tuesday, time will have looped around on itself like a snake consuming its tail. On that day the can from the future will stand in place of the one from the past, which will be missing because I must have forgotten to cart it out to the street.

Dr Ekman's Implement

Conversation at mealtime often turns to the beloved Dr Ekman, inventor of the companion to knife, fork and spoon, but which no one knows how to use. Children are not allowed to handle it except when setting the table, and it sits beside their plates, undeniably handsome, like a token of faith in their future pleasures and responsibilities. At first they had to be reminded where to place it, but at that time even the parents were unsure since habit was not yet ingrained, and the mother might have consulted a relative or friend on the phone or debated the issue with her husband before setting it next to the knife, on the right-hand side of the bowl or plate, following the custom. And so a buzz of talk would start even before the family sat down to enjoy their meal.

It's not much longer than any other piece of silverware, but has handles on each end, or at least the suggestion of two grips in its pommel-like protrusions, so inviting to the open palm. This means of course that it can be grasped by both hands at once, something deeply frowned upon, however, and yet almost irresistible to the diner. Like children, then, grownups have frustrations of their own, though the word is perhaps too harsh since the habit of self-denial has become more like second nature, and with the added gratification that comes with a newly-mastered sublimation. This fine turn of self-control and etiquette has a further benefit, moreover, since the tool is very dangerous, with its razor-edged serrations that curl around the shaft, meeting the fingers where they never expect. If that seems at times a disadvantage, this is forgiven Dr Ekman, inventor of so many useful things for the kitchen and home: the carving knife, so marvelously sharp, but which turns blunt when it meets human skin; the pots without handles that can be held with bare hands even when their contents are scalding; and his hot-water device that replaced all teakettles by bringing water to a boil at the flick of a switch. But as for his last invention the doctor left no directives, and it remained after his passing the work that sums up his life and creative genius.

A grandmother at the dinner table sometimes pities the poor Hindus who eat with their hands or the Chinese who remain content with their chopsticks. If they are chided for such jawing no one begrudges their pride, since much of the world has also laid claim to Dr Ekman's genius. Unlike the fork, credited to Italy and the court of France, Dr Ekman's invention is claimed by Germany, his homeland, by Sweden, his adopted country, by Denmark, where he developed his designs, by Canada and the United States, where he launched his empire, and by Japan, where he refined much of his work, inspired by the metalwork of the age of the Shoguns. In his final years Dr Ekman is said to have traveled in Papua and Dahomey, apparently to study sacred artifacts and ceremonial objects, whose traces some can detect in his wonderful tool. If this is so, could the meaning of those rites, assuming one condoned them, be passed on even to those who do not know their purpose?

A bauble? A conversation piece? Surely not, since Dr Ekman's invention, as everyone knows, arrived at the dawn of this age of peace, when all wars have ended, swords hammered into ploughshares.

Out of Body

That got my attention, he thought, as his head came away from his body. He'd been trying to ignore her all day, and now this. But in fact his mind was already on other things. We'll never leave this apartment, he realized. How would they make the move, how could they get settled in a new neighborhood with him headless, deformed, a freak even to the misfits of the Lower East Side? Imagine the pointing, the staring. At least they knew him here in SoHo, he had what's called a network of friends, people she loved but who he wanted to get away from, truth be told, though now it looked like he'd be needing them for basic support. And so, decapitated, was he finally coming around to her side?

They had always argued, always, e.g. about that loft on the Bowery. We should of bought that place, she never stopped crabbing. We could of partitioned it, made rent to live on. But no, because of him they had to keep a step ahead of gentrification, living like rats while their friends stayed put and watched their equity bloom. Downwardly mobile. No kids yet either. There were a million reasons to fight, but it had never been quite this bad, he realized, when he saw her lift the hatchet and bring it down on his neck. It was without warning, if not entirely unprovoked, like Cato in The Pink Panther, or was it Kato Kaelin, of O.J. Simpson fame? As they always say about the moment of death, his life was passing before his eyes, mostly scenes of marital strife scrambled up with tabloid violence and slapstick comedy – To the moon, Alice! – and he thought for an addled moment he was blacking out. But it was just a jog in the brain as his head thumped onto the floorboards.

I'm sorry, she said, cradling his head in her lap and stanching the blood with a pillow, one his mother had gifted them, he couldn't help noticing. His body sat bolt upright in the armchair opposite like a house guest pressed into watching a family squabble. The damage was bad but he still thought he might have won the argument since she had clearly gone too far this time. He tried to stiffen himself against her mollifying caresses and was surprised he didn't have the heart, then was surprised at his surprise since, of course, he didn't.

How could it have come to this, he asked himself. A wave of tenderness flowed over him and he reflected on the feeling, curious but dry-eyed. Was it self-pity? Slave morality? And what if she exploited his weakness? He tried to take stock of his position before all was lost, but at the very thought of loss he just caved in like a schoolgirl admitting a crush, and that was it, he was gone. He felt his last chance escaping him and watched the decisive moment float away, as if too distracted by drowning to clutch at a tendered grapnel.

But having lost everything, he suddenly felt everything was OK. The arguments stopped, he no longer stomped out or slammed the door but considered things in a new light, calmly, deliberately, resting in her lap or in the crook of his body's arm as it attended to his needs and hers like a silent butler. Still, it was odd at first, so he thought they should cleave to routine as best as they could. One day he and his body made off to the local bookshop where he wanted to look up a few things, the story of the Headless Horseman, for instance. But the Knickerbocker was no help and neither were any books on the age of the guillotine, though he lost himself for a long while in David's sketch of Marie Antoinette trundling to the scaffold. Mouth turned down at the sides. Resignation? Defiance? As for Saint Denis, the story was interesting but apocryphal, sadly. So he was a one-off. Meanwhile, his body paced the aisles like a racehorse pawing the dirt and generally made a show of its impatience. Then instead of going home it whisked them to the neighborhood gym, filled out a membership with the dumbstruck cashier, and went straight down to the weight room, swinging him like a bowling ball.

A brainiac his entire life, he couldn't recall ever setting foot in a gym. His body was making up for lost time. At the bench press it needed no spotter, and risking none of the usual hazards pumped away until closing time. You might have said it had something in mind, but it was just a machine answering to specs and without any neurotic meddling on his part. Within a week it started to bulk out and even seemed taller than he remembered, an effect perhaps of his reduced perspective. Knuckle-draggers ducked in their presence as if near the blades of an invisible Sikorski.

But it's amazing how novelty can trump fear and disgust. They became popular. Their first night in a bar it was nothing but bugging eyes. His body gripped his head under its arm like a motorcylist with a helmet, and forgoing the prop of a drink leaned nonchalant against the bar, simply waiting. He felt his body exert something like gravitational force on all the women in the place, celestial bodies would be no exaggeration, they were two blocks from NYU. And he was caught in that force too, but like a moon in a collapsed orbit. So began a period of completely reckless philandering, which he watched from the floor, among discarded clothing or propped on a hope chest, but most often abandoned on the way to the bedroom, and mercifully few times slung into a hamper or dropped inconsiderately on the bathroom floor, in which case the scenes of lovemaking would sometimes be punctuated by a roommate's bloodcurdling shrieks. Strange to say, he felt closer than ever to that body, even when marveling at its exploits, or rather, unmoved but always interested, observing the budding of its separate life.

As for his wife, why did she put up with it? The late nights, the early mornings, and worse, the shaggy afternoon returns when doubt must have crept into her mind that they would ever come home at all? She was turning motherly. After all, she had created them in a way, and she put up with that wild month that seemed an eternity like the parent of adolescent boys. And when they finally came home to stay he realized his body had been schooling itself in feminine pleasure like a student cramming for finals. In the bedroom she didn't make the gesture he would have expected, that of a faithless woman turning over a family portrait, by setting him aside or covering his face with a towel. No, he watched. And it was interesting. Interesting.

Afterward, when his body turned over on its now superfluous pillow, they talked. She glowed with pleasure, and didn't hide it, not needing to. She gushed about the parts she had liked best, and he could only concur, yes, that was good, that was just the thing. He was touched that she confided in him, and, musing, reflected on his lack of jealousy as if consulting some obsolete manual or a tourist guide to Gondwanaland. They were like girlfriends, but without rivalry, or like a pet and its owner who by some miracle had found a perfectly equal footing. Sometimes they cast their minds back to the proverbial ball and chain and the so-called bonds of love, but all that seemed incredibly distant now they had slipped through the loophole. Only once he said, not out of coyness but just to air his thoughts, which were as much his as hers, You know, there are things I could do too…? She just shook her head sensibly, and he felt no more jealousy or spite than a child whose friend has turned down a lick of her lollipop.

They never tired of conversation, and whatever the topic they would circle around that fixed center of their attention, the precious uniqueness of their love. How to qualify it? They never tired of that question either, and as if drawing from a deep, unruffled well they brought up only the most limpid, cool and refreshing nourishment for the soul. If he feigned some pique at times it was only to get her to show her teeth. Levity, levity. But how to refer to his body when it was there, sleeping, or even when it was awake, waiting as it often did like a dog by the front door? *It*, he said at first, then followed her lead in calling it *Him*, *He*. But then what was he, who could never be a third person in their conversations but was always a third party to their sex?

Life went on. For endless afternoons they walked down the streets and through the shabby parks of their familiar neighborhood. He observed her hand squeezed tight in the hand of his body. Interesting. The friendly bump of thighs as their bodies matched their pace. Interesting. Head crushed tight against the side of his body, joggling slightly, like an infant in those slings favored by the hipster cognoscenti he used to despise. Interesting, interesting, now that all was forgiven and that he was even forgetting what there might have been to forgive.

He was gaga, he had to admit. In love, as if falling, always falling, he loved it, he loved his body.

Belayed

I must have circled the block four times before I gave it up and tried the boulevard, then turned without thinking down a dark residential street where a familiar shape drifted into view. Its tall crested outline was both bigger and smaller than I remembered: mansionesque in a shabby Victorian way but stranded in a corner of the world that looked scaled down somehow. My room faced the blackened cedar shakes of the house next door; in other rooms and at the top of the stairs you could see right out to the Golden Gate. By late afternoon the fog would punch through the gap in the headlands and cross the bay, swamping Berkeley in a chill that made you want to hole up indoors. I winced as an expression came back to me: *brillig*, what emo sophomores called this time of day if we meant to start some drinking.

I was going to be late meeting the others. None of the group hailed from that era but Cindy, and then only indirectly, as girlfriend of a housemate, all of three weeks. After college our paths crossed now and then but less and less often; we'd both moved to the suburbs, in opposite directions. Even so she never looked surprised to see me again. When we bumped into each other at the supermarket she invited me out with her friends, nonchalant, as if we'd talked just the day before, though I was sure it had been more like a year. I almost started a mental calculation on the point. The car was idling and I was still staring up at the house when a girl appeared backlit in the door frame. She suddenly leaped down the steps and ran straight at me. My first thought was that I must know her, that she recognized me, idiotic of course. Then with a jolt she'd accuse me of stalking. Instead there was the glint of a key as she ducked into the car in front and pulled away from a miraculous empty space.

Trees that never went bare. I had trouble getting used to it. Winter nights they threw dark blooms of shadow on the street and you'd want to roll down the window as if cruising in midsummer then remember not. No place in mind but needing to push out and away from the stoplights that dose your flight, you'd end up on long avenues flanked by hangars and foundries then houses: unkempt, bedrooms exposed, but rooted there. A curtain might pull back as the car went by. On straight, endless San Pablo Avenue the bleary orange glare of sodium lights flickered over the windshield and shaded the gap-toothed rows of shuttered storefronts. When those petered out the suburbs lay off ahead and the string of lights led away into dark shapelessness. Then it was time to turn around.

With all it brought to mind I knew I'd regret having to come back and see that looming silhouette again. It was just as hard to park in those days, and when the street sweepers came you had to move your car the night before or swallow a citation. My habit was to put it off until morning, but I'd always try to catch a few more minutes of sleep, picturing an enforcer already climbing the sidewalk with the rising sun.

When I finally joined them at the bar Cindy was in the middle of a story that couldn't be interrupted. She didn't understand it and she wanted an explanation, one she could shake her head at. Or she understood it well enough but there was still a scrap of doubt she hung on to with a rising pitch of desperation. It didn't help the others were only half listening, but that escaped her too.

It was last summer. She was hiking with Marco, and since they'd gotten a late start it looked like they were going to reach the peak around sunset. That was not a problem in itself. June days are long, twilight tenacious, and the sky was clear so the evening would be bright enough for the return. The only people they met were making their way back down, which can be unnerving when night is beginning to fall. In fact they'd already missed the sunset, they learned from the last hikers. They were on the east side of the mountain, I think she forgot to mention.

Once above the trees the slopes pitched skyward like the

hump of some giant dozing creature. Dim light, but not to worry. In any case they had flashlights, not that flashlights are best for a rocky descent. She seemed about to get lost in details, but picked up again and went on. The final stretch was like climbing an endless stairway, she said, heads down, trudging, until they noticed the light had begun to increase, as if dawn were breaking. Was she hyperventilating? They stopped to catch their breath. No, it was true, the sky was steadily brightening, soft, milky, diaphanous. An aurora? Or maybe they had walked straight through the night, unconscious or dreaming? They continued upward, eyes on the sky, marveling at the incongruous daybreak.

Next came the most poetic part, but it was lost on Sarah, the city girl, Joanie, the ditz, and Stan, who was eying the college girls, another distraction, though come to think of it there was a fireplace at the far end of the pub, always good for spinning a yarn. So the poetic part: she said she had a sudden irrational sense the mountain was floating in the air, and that the sun had swiftly passed beneath their feet, was coming out the other side, like a cat slinking under the table. My metaphor, but full disclosure: I was obsessed with the idea of playing footsie with her. Marco, thank God he wasn't here for once, had his own theory about light diffraction or the receding horizon she was willing to entertain up to a point. I gather they argued but she skipped over that. In any case the magic lasted only a short while, twenty minutes tops, and when they reached their destination it was a prosaic world they beheld, the ordinary glory of amazing vistas and human solitude under an unmistakably darkening sky.

By which time I was having an argument with myself. Her story had conjured something different for me: the painting of a boulder in the clouds, a castle and battlements perched on top, walls and towers tiny because apparently remote, all hewn from aerial bedrock. A perennial favorite, that picture, it summed up a lifetime in miniature, from high-school *D&D* to skulking college goth. Did she remember – or know it without remembering? I had a nagging suspicion I couldn't nail down I'd seen that poster in my housemate's room when Cindy was dating him. I wanted to know, but I had no way to be sure, that it was tacked to the wall separating our rooms, or that we shared, the wall that thumped like a drum when she spent the night, their bed being right up against it, or against the picture itself – why not? – that met her full in the face even as she tried to muffle the sounds, knowing of course, since it was the middle of the night, that someone was there, that it was me on the other side of the castle, the clouds, the never-spilling breakers. I held the thought and stood mentally in their room, trying to picture the furnishings, but I was stuck, distracted as always by the dazzling view across the bay, beyond the bridge, out onto the ocean where you could barely make out those strange sawtoothed islands in the haze.

The Farallones, I remembered the name later, wincing again, tipsy, single and stumbling to the car. Something else came to me on the way, a piece of trivia from Art History. The painter Magritte never gave titles to his pictures; he hosted a salon and showed them to friends so they could suggest names of their own, the more random the better. I snorted at the thought but it came out as a fit of coughing.

Did you make it back OK? Joanie asked, as if just waking up. Obviously that part was not worth telling. The story was over. Cindy's anxious tone had subsided, and if she was disappointed with the audience it didn't show, besides which her story must have gained something in the process since she seemed to hold it even closer like a private treasure. That was her in a nutshell. I could have folded her in my arms then and said I understood, I understood everything. Impossible, of course, she never went for the bookish types. She was far away from me, unconcerned about the others, and her sweet face, no longer young but heart-breaking still, had the calm self-absorption of an egg-like gibbous moon.

News from Livermore

So we live forever, the question's settled, or nearly forever, and there the problems start. The churches are folding, we're no longer at each others' throats, but the hereafter occupies us more than ever. When Gallatin announced his discovery that day in June it was like New Year's Eve across the world. What followed is a hangover that will apparently never end.

The pessimists were already brooding as we lifted our glasses to eternal life. They were wondering what we all do now: whether to remember this moment or to simply enjoy it, to bank on the eternal return or to try to live in the present. We were suddenly rich beyond all imagining, but were like thieves glued to the spot, loaded down with a freighter's cargo.

The news was simple: we'll relive our lives. And with that came the all-important caveat: we relive what we remember. Gallatin had won the Nobel Prize a decade earlier with his discovery that time is not linear but spiral; both continuous like a line and looping like a circle, it returns always to each point on its path, but with an incremental difference that keeps it from ever closing the orbit. For the next ten years his team at Livermore Labs ran tests that led to their discovery of the Anomaly: a bridge in time allowing researchers to span the tiny gap to the next ring of the spiral. To illustrate this with a metaphor Gallatin said it was like skipping the needle on a record player. But in this case (and we all recall his kindly smile) he said that rather than break the rhythm and the melody, the needle kept playing the identical tune in a second temporal realm. Standing at the bristly rostrum and surrounded by cameras, he then spelt out the implications the spiral had for every living being on Earth. It was a tall order, but he carried it off with memorable composure. He told us we must imagine a record of an immense circumference, whose first ring is the length of our lives, and we must imagine that what is engraved on the next ring is the sum of our remembered experiences. We'll relive those experiences, he assured us, the next time around. I wonder why it didn't occur to me then that a record's rings grow smaller as they near the center. Of course we all know the reason now.

Because in fact our lives are shorter at the next turn of the spiral, for the simple reason that we don't remember everything we live through. Whole swaths of early childhood are lost to memory as we fast-forward to adolescence and beyond. At a press conference a few weeks later, Gallatin had the fine sense to invoke Joyce's *A Portrait of the Artist*, in which Stephen Dedalus' earliest years, from his first inklings of self-awareness up to his school days, are spanned in a mere page and a half. Likewise, we will be born again, but we'll live in a time flow of our own making, jumping from moment to moment, often from week to week, if not month to month or more. We'll relive our memorable hours and our lives will come back as a story, he cheerfully said, like Joyce's novel. A reporter cut in to point out that a novel can be read in a sitting. He wasn't the only one to raise questions that verged on heckling. By that time, of course, Gallatin's discovery weighed on us like a curse.

We started to live as collectors of memories, afraid to lose anything that escaped our notice. A person at the bus stop had the jumpy look of a thief, furtive eyes darting from side to side and falling onto ordinary objects as if deciphering their significance, or peering into the distance to make out things that shouldn't have concerned them but now seemed to pose an inimical menace. We were all eyes, all ears, aware that a blink of your lashes swept an eraser across the landscape. Behind your head there loomed an obliterating force like the Earth's cone of shadow in space. People whirled around as if answering a call no one else could hear, or stopped dead in their tracks for no evident reason. You might have thought we'd become poets, fingering the grain of the wood, scenting the air, weighing our words, but eternity left us frenzied, rummaging in things we missed taking for granted.

Of course there were things we truly cherished and were glad to hold on to, but in our moments of greatest joy we were busy consigning our orgasms to the record. It would be a small sin if our minds turned inward to plumb the depths of our feelings, so long neglected. More or less the opposite was the case, though. What good was a moment of pleasure if it came back floating in a haze, without consistency, without detail, without context? And the subsequent turn, would it be as impalpable as a dream? We had sex with the lights on, wild-eyed, distracted. A mother holding her baby would worry its fingers and toes as if afraid that some were missing, then stare at it with a distant look as if forgetting its face there and then. How could you not stop in dumb amazement when watching a child take its first steps, knowing that the living scene had no second chance except in your own stash of memories? Sleeping people seemed to hibernate, even when lying on a blanket in the sun, and nothing was more uncanny than watching someone nod off for a nap.

We've always known that moments of grief stick best in the mind. The insight now raised a host of anxious questions: should we provoke pain to assure the permanent work of memory? How often can you pinch a child to keep it alert, as if warding off coma for someone with a concussion?

When a likeness of calm returned, many found comfort in narrowing the circle of their days. They wouldn't leave the house except to pace the yard, to study the cut of a leaf, to recite the names of trees. They'd scold the children, stop them from playing, and hold up a bulb for them to squirrel away in their heads. A stranger passing in the road would appear to them as a ghost. Inside, they'd make an endless inventory of their things so as to be sure of coming back to a familiar place. But like a splinter in the brain, they'd always remember Gallatin at the podium and relive the moment that has become the story of our lives.

There's no blaming the hermits, the alcoholics, the hysterics.

The promise of repetition makes the present redundant in advance, like the first rehearsal of a play that can't be cancelled or a book that has to be constantly rememorized. It's exhausting to confront crowds, the seashore or a splendid view when your work of mental description almost requires you to bring them into being, not like a painter at his canvas, but like a filmmaker without a camera. Years after Gallatin's death we recalled his famous invocation of *The Portrait of the Artist*. Maybe it's true, as he suggested, that we've finally become the autobiographers of our lives. But Joyce's late work was nearly illegible.

I've come to a decision, though I can't remember when I made it. As in all important moments, the eye seeks out things on which to impress your thoughts.

A cardinal is perched on the bare tree outside. His legs grip tight to a black twig. The branch extends toward the trunk, gradually widens, then fades into a blur, then into sheer absence. The branch is floating in the air. I must have assumed it once joined a tree rooted in the ground, somewhere I can't see, somewhere I never saw, under the achromatic snow.

Time Code

The day his mother died he meant to visit her at the hospital in the afternoon. She had been in a bad way all week, but nothing suggested it was so serious until she had an incident just before midday. At the time they were on the road to Greg and Alison's house for a garden party. Somehow he'd forgotten the cell phone, which he didn't realize until they were already on the highway. Blame it on the kids, they'd been driving him and Susan crazy all morning. He could have called the hospital from Greg's place but didn't get around to it. Instead he picked up the phone when they got back to the house and found that ominous list of messages. Mother was gone.

They'd told her he must be on his way to the hospital. They'd told her he must have gotten the messages and was in too much of a rush to call back. It's illegal to talk on the cell phone in the car. He was probably parking downstairs as they spoke. Was that him coming down the hall? No, it was just another grim-faced nurse. So her last thoughts had been about her favorite son. She might even have thought he could save the day. Maybe she hung on a bit longer with that hope in spite of the nervous tone in his brother and sister's voices. Or maybe the waiting had been too much for her in the end.

He would never live it down. He should have been there when it happened, and he was tortured by the thought that not being there was why it happened when it did. A simple phone call and the sound of his voice might have kept her hanging on. He was only minutes away, after all. But the moment passed him by. Later of course he went over everything with his brother and sister. Time of death. He insisted on knowing to the minute. They were each at the bedside, holding her hands. What had she said at the end? He was almost afraid to ask. It wasn't about him at least, but that could have meant she'd given up on him already, which made his stomach slump again.

The garden party hung over his memory of that day like a reproach. They even shunned Greg and Alison for a month, in spite of their condolences, a couple of unanswered phone calls and then a card and flowers a few days later. Finally Susan said, Enough, it's not their fault, and she set up a play date for the kids for the following week. Then he remembered the camcorder, whose battery would need recharging. When he flipped it on he found a recording of the garden party, the very afternoon his mother died. He had taught Ally how to use it a few days earlier, but he hadn't noticed she'd picked it up from the picnic table, while Greg, Alison, Susan and he were chatting on the lawn. Ally was filming the other kids playing, with a good steady hand, no jumpy pans, and standing quietly where no one noticed her. Ally's older brother Tommy had cobbled together an invention and she was following his antics with the camera. His eye sunk down to the time code at the bottom of the screen. A feeling of nausea almost doubled him over. It was a quarter to one in the afternoon, barely a minute after his mother died.

The time code showed that Ally's little film ran for a couple minutes. He could hardly bring himself to rewind the recording. He was about to find out exactly what had been going on when Mother expired, while he, oblivious, was sitting in a lawn chair, beer in hand, talking with his friends, one eye on the kids. You could hear the voices of the adults in the background and the TV murmuring during the half-time break. He braced himself. What if he heard himself guffawing at that exact moment? Or making some coded dirty remark? He had to know, even if it meant he'd bring down a curse.

Tommy had geared up a clever little trick with his electric tractor. It was flipped upside down, and with a length of string he'd gotten God knows where he'd turned the wheels into a motorized spool. On the end of the string he attached one of the girls' dolls, it must have been Sally's, to judge from her screams of frustrated delight. The dog sniffed at the doll when it hit a thick patch of grass, then jumped away when the doll popped back up again. He was watching the time code. This is when Mother died.

He cued the sequence back and the doll crept like an hysteric through the grass, tumbling and twitching as she pulled her cord behind her. Sally's screams sounded like coughing hiccups. That was grotesque enough. But what he was looking for was in the background: an outburst in the middle of the adults' conversation.

It was Susan's voice, barely rising above Alison's, who was apparently telling a story. Susan had said, Oh no, and hearing that on the tape made his hair stand on end. Then he figured she must have been watching the kids' pranks. But suddenly he remembered.

Alison had been telling a story about a day she and Greg were heading to lunch in town and they passed a police car on the bridge to Pasadena. There was just enough time to glance sideways as they drove by and they saw an officer perched on the balustrade, looking over the edge. It isn't called the Suicide Bridge for nothing. The stricken look on a bystander's face made it clear someone had just jumped. This is the point when Susan said, Oh no. But that wasn't the moment mother died. And in fact Alison was telling the story for another reason.

A colleague of Greg's was in the car with them, Alison said, and he'd been in the middle of telling a story when they got onto the bridge. He stopped talking when they saw the scene at the balustrade, and all of them, of course, made some comment or other on the tragic scene. A helicopter was heading their way. But before they'd even reached the other side of the bridge the colleague picked up his story again, and Alison said she could never forgive him for that. This is when Mother died.

And what did he say then? What did he have to say just after Mother died? What deep thoughts, what symbolic statement crossed his lips at that moment? He remembered exactly. He wanted to know what was so important about the colleague's story that he couldn't let go of it. Surely it was more than chit-chat? But he didn't wait for the answer because he also wanted to know how much time one should grant to a complete stranger, whose death they had not seen, and which they had only assumed, before going on with your life? A moment of silence? Thirty seconds? It was almost as if he were provoking Alison, though he couldn't for the life of him imagine why. And wincing as he recalled this, he remembered holding back from saying something to the effect that people die every day, even if we don't see it from our cars. Offscreen and unspoken, barely even hatched in his brain, that thought was mercilessly captured by the tape as well. But his mother wasn't on his mind then. At that point she was only sick and hopefully recovering, for all he knew.

So then, in a strange, even tone, like an insurance agent denying a claim, Alison began telling the story the colleague had been telling on the bridge. This was also on the tape, just a murmur in the background, as Tommy was rescuing the doll from under the wheels of his tractor, Sally frantically hopping behind. The colleague was saying that he'd given his girlfriend an engagement ring, and his girlfriend asked him, right after oohing and aahing, whether it was a blood diamond or not, but he didn't even know the meaning of the question. Needless to say, it was the beginning of the end for them.

Playing back the tape, he recognized the tinny sound of music coming from the TV at that moment. No one had been paying attention, probably, but in retrospect it explained how Alison got started on her story, with that other story inside, and the gap in the middle, and the unforgivable blunder. It was the soundtrack to an advertisement for a jewelry store, featuring a well-known piece of classical music. He'd seen the ad a million times: a sixty-second spot in which a young man presents a diamond ring to his girlfriend. They're standing on a bridge, it screams Tuscany, and the sun is low over the romantic vista. Then, a cut, the couple is much older, and she makes the same gesture of fingering her ring before the two of them turn away from the camera, which swings high upward to encompass the view. In the middle of the ad the music pauses briefly and you see a bespectacled jeweler intent on his craft putting the final touches on his token of immortality. This is the moment Mother died.

He wasn't quite done torturing himself. Hunched over with his ear to the speaker, he listened to a steady drone he mistook at first for Tommy's tractor. The humming noise rose and started drowning out the other sounds before the clip abruptly ended. It seemed like a train bearing down with obliterating purpose, but it could only be a jet or a helicopter passing overhead. He had a moment of dizzyness, because with his eyes closed it seemed the craft was on its way to the bridge, maybe even filming the advertisement, which he knew was impossible, but for a long moment he was drawn into that hush when everyone is looking but would rather have looked away.

When a plane crosses the sun, a flicker can hit you like a missed heartbeat. The moment of his mother's death had cast a blot that wouldn't move off, as if the plane spreadeagled in the sky had come to a dead stop. What to do with the memory card? He'd never look at it again. File it away in a drawer, unlabeled, like a piece of beach glass you don't remember picking up. Someone might record over it one day. No, that was a lie, he knew that now it had become an object, mute, invisible and unforgiving, somewhere in his inventory of things he'd always keep a place for the moment of his mother's death.

After the funeral he pressed his sister for more about her final hour. Mother was in pain, his sister told him, and she kept going back to her happy place. She talked about the garden in the house where she grew up. There was a little lawn between the trees, and her grandmother, who loved to sit in the sun, got up from her chair every so often to follow the moving patch of sunlight. Their mother, probably Ally's age then, learned to tell time with that lawn chair. Eleven o'clock, twelve o'clock, one o'clock, two o'clock, as she helped her grandmother drag it across the grass. That must have been in the thirties. It was before cell phones, helicopters, camcorders and time codes.

Visitation

I doze off as my wife is reading. She turns the pages quietly, considerately, knowing I'm a light sleeper, but I'm aware she's making that effort, which keeps me up for a spell. If it's a book she's reading you can count a minute or two between each turn of the page, less if she's browsing a magazine, though she usually spares me that constant rustling and settles down with a story, or is it an essay, no telling. I might have married a pious woman, missal in hand, fingering pages thin as a watermark, silent, translucent, immaterial.

I had a dream and woke up again. She set her reading aside with a distracted look, but when I finished rambling her face was strangely serious. She said I should write the dream down, just how I told it, then send it off to a magazine (she pulled out a copy of *The New Yorker*). It was if she had said, Go back to sleep, dummy. But I put on my robe, went into the other room and transcribed the dream, after which I sent it to *Harper's* and got an acceptance letter improbably soon, about a month later.

It was too easy. All I had to do was shake myself from bed and plant a pen in my fist. I would write to the magazine of my choice and say, Dear Editors, here is another dream I had, I hope you will find it of interest. Generous checks would follow. But of course I sent out no other stories, I woke up to dross like anyone. Maybe I should have been gratified at seeing my name in a top venue, but I knew my publication was a fluke and I had the nagging sense it was undeserved. Afterward I could never muster any creativity on my own account. In the end, I suppose, I had only aspired to take dictation.

At the time I had a stint with the college where I had graduated five years earlier (B.A., English). It was no joy returning to that campus when my wife and other classmates had moved on to real careers, but it being summertime I didn't risk running into my former professors and I wouldn't have to play the aging townie to a new crop of innocents. The library was getting renovated with a windfall from a tech industry alum, and my job was to stock books and cart them to the new mobile shelving system – the "coed compactor," as the circ-desk guy put it, an allusion he wouldn't expand on. The head librarian hovered around the apparatus buffing imaginary scratches, appearing out of nowhere if I put my hands on a lever, so I tried to stay out of his way, preferably alone downstairs. The work stretched out longer than needed because I dawdled and daydreamed, reading whole books standing in the aisles or even sprawled on the floor. Once I heard steps somewhere and the lights went out. "There's someone down here," I called out. "Sorry, Someone," they called back.

Every day was like Sunday, idle and empty. Passing by a dorm one morning I noticed a few shelves of books had been left behind in a room. Apparently the cleaning crew had not gotten to disposing of them yet. The next morning they were still there, so after work I let myself into the room (unlocked, on the ground floor) and looked over the shelves. A number of the books I knew to be quite valuable, including an almost complete set of Sigmund Freud's works in the clothbound *Standard Edition*. Those were too heavy to carry, but I helped myself to other volumes, for some reason taking only paperbacks, mostly respectable literary classics, but also criticism, history and philosophy. I made a fair amount of cash selling them at the bookstore downtown.

No doubt some maid would make off with the rest. It must be a boon to the cleaning crew, I thought, when students clear out at year's end without even bothering to pack up all their stuff. A rich upperclassman must have had the room with the leftover books. I knew the type. What wasn't disposable for a kid with their father's Am Ex itching to fly away somewhere? I had noticed there were a few things still hanging in the dorm room's closet and at least one piece of furniture that didn't look like school property. But the more I thought about the remaining books the more I felt they shouldn't fall into a housekeeper's hands. My motives were not so mercenary, I reasoned, since I meant to keep some of the books for myself. Things looked the same at the dorm the next morning, and at the end of the workday I picked up a good pile, half for the bookstore and half for my collection. I told my wife they were surplus the library was letting go. That needless reflex should have tipped me off.

Because someone had been in the room, I realized, the next time I went by. The curtains were pulled closed, though the door was still unlocked. One or two objects had been shifted, which I chalked up to a housekeeper making an inventory or a first pass at cleaning. As for the bedroom, I never looked in, only the books mattered to me. I had a backpack and carried off a good haul worth about $50 in trade.

There remained the Freud, which kept me from sleeping that night. If in fact the cleaning crew was snooping around the books might disappear the next day. I decided to visit the dorm before work, taking a rolling suitcase, the kind with a telescoping handle, more than ample for those 24 volumes. The bag was kind of incriminating and I asked myself which was less conspicuous: lugging it straight across the lawn or rolling it nonchalant on a zigzag course? I opted for the unaesthetic shortcut. I let myself into the dorm as stealthily as possible and started quietly packing the books, one ear trained on the path outside where groundskeepers would go by, though it was still so early that nobody was on campus. But a sound came from inside the bedroom, as if right behind my head. I froze in mid-motion. There was a kind of groan, or a heavy sigh, and a sleepy voice said, "Sarah?" Then I heard a rustling noise. I was about to bolt out the door but balked when my eyes fixed on the luggage tag sporting my name and address in my wife's neat cursive hand, the letters thoughtfully protected from the elements by a clear plastic window. There was no way to run with the bag and no way to leave it unless I tore off that tag, but I could plainly see two shiny rivets attaching it to the suitcase with permanent intent. Ever the English major, for a millisecond I thought how the word "rivet" is used to describe someone stuck in place or a story you can't tear yourself away from. I was still half bent over the open suitcase, paralyzed and ridiculous like someone caught by a searchlight, when I finally heard the long slow breathing of a sleeping person. I crept over to the bedroom door and peeked in. Unlike the front room it showed all the signs of current occupancy. And someone was in the bed, turned toward the wall.

It must be a professor, I realized, likely some bachelor, in any case a younger man, to judge from his hair, an adjunct teaching with the skeleton crew of faculty in the college summer seminars. There was no sign of any woman. He was basically camped out, untidily, though his room was one of the better ones on campus, a real suite, with views out onto the green where the sun was just coming up.

The next part is what I don't get. After holding a frozen pose and watching the sunlight climb the wall, I began carefully taking down those handsome volumes of Freud's, pale blue dust jackets intact, and stacking them in the suitcase. Only two of the *Standard Edition* were missing, maybe they were at the young professor's bedside. I considered stalking up and slipping them away while he slept. It seemed logical at that moment, or inevitable, like an act obeying one of Newton's laws of physical motion.

I remember every detail from that summer, right down to the feel of the wax on the library woodwork and the smell of stale dust and the paper slowly oxidizing ("burning," the circ guy would say). I have a spatial memory, but with all the back-and-forth in the stacks some episodes got out of place. I can't recall when I overheard the story about the professor, a poet in the creative writing program, whose wife learned of his affair with a student and kicked him out of the house. For the whole summer he lodged in a dorm room with nothing but the contents of a suitcase, his life an open parenthesis. Meanwhile the wife was messing with him, they said.

I replaced the two missing volumes with store credit. Their dust jackets are older, so more faded than the others, which is a bit annoying, but on the whole the set makes quite an impression, especially to guests at the dinner table where they preside over our talk. Inevitably someone always says, Paging Dr Freud, which is obviously no great feat of wit, and besides, no one ever takes a volume down from the shelf.

A story goes with those books, and my wife made me tell it whenever the chance came up. A retired Italian professor, the husband of an old alum, came to donate them personally to the school, but the library already had two full sets. We talked for hours in the stacks. What a life he had led, it was a pleasure to embroider on it. He had known Primo Levi before he was sent to the camps. He spent the war years on the Azores, a place I'd always wanted to see. He trained the first students to do psycho-analysis among the Tupinambá, partnered with Carl Jung on a study of Hopi myths and tripped with Carlos Castañeda in the Sonoran Desert. All my schooling went into those stories. They were the highlight of dinner conversation until I finally tired of them, not wanting to become like one of those oldsters who trundle out the same yarns, suspiciously well-rehearsed, at every occasion. Guilt is a fickle muse. Regardless, my wife likes the books, they go with our pillows.

After the End

It was so bad that people were rendered speechless. An attack out of the blue, so much violence, so many victims, no need for details. When the initial shock was past and as they groped their way back to a semblance of life, some tried talking then thought better. So a second silence descended, stifling the impulse to speak, then the memory of that impulse, and finally even the memory of that memory, leaving us with nothing but the present moment and the stinking evidence of our survival.

Was it shame that stupefied us? Did the word still rattle with some faint meaning, like a token of the past in a shoebox? No, all words scattered loose, they'd lost their resonance, and if they came back to mind at times each one retained only a trace of its useless uniqueness that we'd chew over in silence, rediscovering in that mute activity something of their original virtue. Were we sullen? We may have looked it, but the word now lacking, the emotion was too. Or perhaps appearing sullen and realizing it, someone may have reflected on the word, if reflection is the word, and turning it over in his mind it would have appeared to him like a leaf, say, a leaf different from all others, with veins that resembled in miniature the tree on which it had grown, but that no longer existed.

Not to exaggerate, trees still grew and thrived, and much of our lives in fact went back to normal. The world is full of buzzing, twangling sounds, only now we heard them like birds without voices. Many of those sounds were recordings from the past, reruns of radio shows or TV programs we watched as much as ever, though eventually they got repetitive and too boring to hold our attention. The newscasters kept their time slots at first and for hours on end did nothing different than us, staring dumbly out from the other side of the screen. Perhaps they might have put their heads in their hands or sighed from time to time? Symbolic gestures, they were no longer tempting.

Many other gestures also fell into disuse. A person who forgot something, then remembered it, and hardly caring but remembering nonetheless, would turn around suddenly in the street and retrace his steps, without the gesture we remember, which we don't care to recall anymore, of a person striking his forehead or stroking his chin, or, less dramatically, slowing down as if musing and coming to a decision, which of course had already been made. It was a relief to have people push you aside rather than appeal to your good graces, since the push was without deeper motive than that of their body in motion, neither greedy, impatient, hostile, or conceited, or feigning impatience to mask hostility, or greedy for your attention but too conceited to avow it, to name just a few combinations from that storehouse of affects that has finally burned to a crisp.

My neighbor climbs onto his roof and sits. He's there at any old time, no more significant than his chimney or the bird that lands on the aerial, perfectly uncaring of the signals caught in its mangled arms. All that's left now is to cope with the mess. Tools in the crud pull out relics we dust off before wiping our hands clean. Books are stocked in the libraries again. We're very good readers, the kind that need no shushing, and we turn the pages carefully, patiently, calmly intent. We live in the present. We've become ghosts, to adopt an expression from your books. We're robots, to rehash a figure from those tired old flicks. We're alive, to resurrect a word from the past, but without the anxiety you gave it now that it's no longer used.

Chances are, when you pick up a book you're reading the words of the dead. Maybe that should be enough to strike a person dumb, but from what I gather it caused no trouble to our forebears. Not that it worries us either, we're past all fuss and bother, but our way of reading draws on the knowledge, or rather the mute testimony burned lately into our flesh. A book expects no response, only our focus. So we pay close attention, with the result that, on this side of the hecatombs, all meanings have become inverted. We've become silent as books, while they chatter on in the face of our impassivity, often about requited love, the everlasting, the end of times, the realms of tranquility. It's not for us to correct them, but we can at least crack a volume and put our face up to an open page.

Incidence

It was a typical renter's tale. He had bought a big mirror to expand the look of his pitifully cramped apartment, but still the space was too tight, crammed with stuff, and he wished he could move everything to the other side of the mirror where he could view it from his empty quarters. As any therapist will tell you, dreams reflect the events of the previous day. He had in fact bought a large mirror that day, meaning to stuff his things on the other side of the glass.

Acknowledgments

A generous grant and residency fellowship from the Albert and Elaine Borchard Foundation allowed me to begin work on these stories. I'd like to thank those who read parts of the manuscript: Dan Katz, Tom Hofheinz, Stefan Mattessich, Connie Samaras, Michelle de Kretser, Rei Terada, Jonathan Hall and Larold Will, as well as my colleagues in the Writing Program at Scripps College. My thanks and compliments to Farley Gwazda, who tackled the illustrations with thoughtfulness and meticulous care. I'd also like to express my gratitude to the editors of the journals where some of these pieces first appeared: Howard Junker, Nam Le, John McAuliffe, and Ed Sugden. Many thanks to Phil Jourdan for his energy, perspicacity and kindness. Thank you, Dina Al-Kassim, for your patience and love.

About the Author

John Culbert was born in Tokyo and raised in Geneva, Switzerland. He is the author of *Paralyses*, winner of the Modern Language Association's Scaglione Prize for French Studies. His short stories have appeared in ZYZZYVA, *Wave Composition*, *The Manchester Review* and *Harvard Review*. He lives in Vancouver, where he teaches in the French Program at the University of British Columbia. This is his first book of fiction.

PERFECT EDGE BOOKS

We live in uncertainty. New ways of committing crimes are discovered every day. Hackers and hit men are idolized. Writers have responded to this either by ignoring the harsher realities or by glorifying mindless violence for the sake of it. Atrocities (from the Holocaust to 9/11) are exploited in cheaply sentimental films and novels.

Perfect Edge Books proposes to find a balanced position. We publish fiction that doesn't revel in nihilism, doesn't go for gore at the cost of substance — yet we want to confront the world with its beauty as well as its ugliness. That means we want books about difficult topics, books with something to say.

We're open to dark comedies, "transgressive" novels, potboilers and tales of revenge. All we ask is that you don't try to shock for the sake of shocking — there is too much of that around. We are looking for intelligent young authors able to use the written word for changing how we read and write in dark times.